D0474840

SOOKIN' BERRIES

Jess Smith

was raised in a large family of Scottish travellers. She is married with three children and six grandchildren. As a traditional storyteller, she is in great demand for live performances throughout Scotland. *Jessie's Journey* was the first book in her autobiographical trilogy, which continued with *Tales from the Tent* and concluded with *Tears for a Tinker*. She has also written a novel, *Bruar's Rest*.

SOOKIN' BERRIES

TALES OF SCOTTISH TRAVELLERS

JESS SMITH

BIRLINN

First published in 2008 by
Birlinn Limited
West Newington House
10 Newington Road
Edinburgh
EH9 1QS

www.birlinn.co.uk

Reprinted 2009

ISBN-13: 978 1 84158 778 3

British Library Cataloguing-in-Publication Data
A catalogue record for this book is available from the British
Library

Set in Bembo and Adobe Jenson at Birlinn

Printed and bound by CPI Cox & Wyman, Reading

Contents

I dedicate this book to Shirley,
who suggested the title

INTRODUCTION

In this book I have tried to share tales I have gathered from my people – the Scottish Travellers, or, as they used to be called, Tinkers. I owe an immense gratitude to the many oral tellers who, without question or doubt, freely handed over their rich treasure-trove of stories which have never been put down on paper until now.

Like torn letters, broken jewellery and odd buttons, the ancient tales were kept in a mind-box, one that was carefully handed down from parent to child. How old the stories are is anybody's guess, and only now have I been given the opportunity to share them with you through this book.

It has given me a great deal of pleasure over the years to be able to relive this collection of rare tales with schoolchildren of varying ages. I do hope you enjoy them too.

In every corner of the earth we find lovers of stories; every one of them has the desire to listen to or to read tales. Each one of them loves to be captivated by a story, one that holds your imagination from the first paragraph to the last. Many of us thrive on unsolved mysteries and dark, fearsome ghost stories. In fact if a story makes our hair rise on our necks and the skin crawl, then that's brilliant

– the more impact the better. Nothing beats curling under a duvet, head and shoulders propped up on feathery pillows, with that favourite book in hand.

Outside the bedroom window a howling gale rips into the darkness of the night; rain-lashed windows add reality to the imaginary beings flitting feverishly from page to page, and fear of the unknown lurking in the shadows adds to the mystery of the book. Your eyelids grow heavy, they feel lead-lined, yet you are still kept awake by the burning desire to know 'who done it', or 'what if the demons get out of the sack?' Was the corn-stacker really a natural human being or something dark and demonic?

§

I have been a gatherer of tales for most of my life, and I suppose it all began when I was a wee girl. I shared a home with parents, seven sisters and a shaggy dog. It could be said that I lived a different sort of life from other children, because 'home' was an old blue bus. We were known as travelling people, and our people, it is believed, had lived in Scotland for two thousand years.

About a generation before I came along, my people lived mainly in the country, weaving baskets, carving horn spoons, making wooden flowers, clothes pegs, brooms and pot scourers created from heather stems bunched together.

As is the way with all ancient skills, progress and technology have brought modern materials and methods, so out went the old ways. With them, the culture of a people and all their customs, language and lifestyle had to go too, to make room for the new. My generation worked in harvesting, potato-gathering, berry-picking and hay-stacking. Heavyduty tractors and diggers with multi-pronged teeth made sure a farmer's fields yielded his desired tonnage of tatties, and as we gathered them up, we suffered from sore backs and wearied legs.

Evening was our favourite time, when Mum, after tidying up

the camp, would whistle to us wherever we were playing and give orders for bed. Hurriedly dressed in jimmy-jams, I'd get a quick wash in a nearby stream and then position myself in a circle of eager faces at the feet of the family storyteller. Before bed we nearly always had stories. With chin resting on scraped knees, elbows tucked in to allow room for another listener, and with a soft breeze whispering round, we were ready to be transported to another world.

The same gentle breeze would stir the finger points of thin branches reaching from a nearby giant oak. They'd touch the top of my head of tousled hair and add extra excitement to what lay ahead. Eyes popping like bubbles I'd listen intently to our storyteller. Tales of darkness, creepiness and disaster with added gore swirled like the smoke of the fire around my straining ears. Tales eddied in my head like whirlpools in a torrent, I'd leave the crackling sticks of our campfire behind and enter into a world of never-ending stories. Fantastic!

In winter time, Traveller children had to go to school. At first I hated being forced to attend, but as I grew older and realised how important it was to be educated and have the same knowledge as other children, I eagerly ran to school. Sadly, bullying of Traveller kids was normal, but I learned to rush around so that the bullies couldn't catch me. Being able to read and write was very important to me.

The law stated that we had to attend school until April and go back there in October. This allowed us to do planting of potatoes, corn, turnips, barley and fruit such as strawberries, raspberries and – in England – apples. We then had a break travelling around the countryside until harvest-time. When this cycle of agriculture was completed, we went back to school, properly dressed in uniforms paid for by the money we made from our hard work. I received my first pay at the tender age of six, being so young that my employer, the farmer, gave it to Mum.

SOOKIN' BERRIES

§

If you are aged round 10 going on 100, then you're a fine age to read, absorb and hopefully remember forever these ancient oral tales of Scotland's travelling people. What I'd like you to do in this book is to come with me on the road, back to those days when it was time to pack up, get going and take the way of our ancestors. I want you to imagine that, as my friend, you are by the campfire listening to and hopefully remembering stories that have been handed down from one generation of Travellers to the other. Some of these tales go so far back in time it is impossible to say how many hundreds of years old they are.

When time came for berry-picking, we arrived at the campsite prepared for us by the fruit farmer, and the first thing we did was seek out other Traveller children. In those days kids from different parts of Scotland would be added to our numbers; all eager to work and play.

As the season went on, tired and weary after picking berries all day under a hot July sun, we couldn't ask for anything better than to sit in the evening gathered around the feet of a certain old man: the magical storyteller.

As we make our way through the tales of this book together, remember that some of the stories are rather creepy, and some can even be considered frightening and horrific! Of course there are lighter tales, some quite funny, and one or two for younger readers. Indeed there is a little bit of what everyone fancies, whether you are young or old. If you are an older reader, settle down with a mug of cocoa. If you're a younger reader and have some homework to finish, then why not do it now, then we'll waste not a minute more. Here's the first tale...

1

A GHOST TALE FROM KINCLADDIE
told by Jimmy Somebody

*Quite when this incident happened, Jimmy, the teller of the tale,
couldn't say exactly. No one had told him in what year he was
born, so his age was always a guess. But on that late autumn day
when I sat in his small pensioner's house in Perth, 'Gateway to
the Highlands', listening like an eager child to his story, it was
apparent from his grey hair and rounded shoulders he'd been on
the earth for some considerable time. My guess is that the events of
this story must have happened around 1920ish.*

My host began to set the scene:

On the outskirts of Dunning, about a mile to the north of the
church tower, we were given permission by a local farmer
to winter-settle in a forested area, known locally as the Ro-
man Wood, in return for doing farm work. Both mother
and father were fairly strong and would find employment
until spring. There were lots of jobs around the farm, and
included piling stones (my sister Katy and I had done that
sometimes), cleaning pigsties and hen huts, stacking hay
for animal feeding, snaring rabbits and many other things

around the farm outhouses. Each year farmers in Perthshire waited eagerly for their Tinker workforce, knowing that without them a farm could easily run into disrepair. From early morning until late at night, my parents both worked hard. While they were at work all day, Granny kept her eye on Katy and me.

People called us wandering Tinkers after our forebears, who mended pots and pans and sharpened kitchen knives and all that kind of stuff. Tinkle, tinkle was the sound we made as we came into villages. We'd fix the pots and bring a wee bit gossip from other parts. That's how we got our name. My parents didn't do pot-mending, but we lived in a tent and when springtime came we moved on, so the name of Tinkers stuck.

Local kids didn't like us, because they thought we were dirty and stole things, but we didn't like them either. Sometimes a nice schoolteacher would come and visit us to see if we wanted to attend school, but because of those hostile kids we didn't go. So me and Katy spent all our time together just playing in the woods or fishing small trout from the burn.

When Granny was small, her tent was built of animal skins; mainly deer hide. But that was in the olden days before more modern materials came in. Dad was lucky enough to buy a big tarpaulin cover from the goods depot at Perth Station, which had been used to protect train-hauled goods from rain damage. It was a deep green colour, the same as grass and trees, and when it was put up deep inside a wood it gave us quite good camouflage.

Dad came back one night after having a few drams with other Tinker folks, and even though he was almost on top of the tent he didn't see it in among the bushes. Katy and me were laughing and playing hide-and-seek with him. He fell over one of the tent ropes and mother told him off for drinking strong alcohol.

For over a week they didn't speak a word to each other, until Granny baked scones. Those scones looked so tasty, Dad took a bite out of one too soon. He burned his mouth and made mother laugh. She gave him a hug and then a drink of water.

One day, after our parents set off for work, we left Granny snoozing by the outside fire and went to explore the forest. For ages we climbed silver birch trees, swinging from top to top like two monkeys. Katy tore her dress and scratched her thigh, so that was the end of that!

Then for a time we followed a small hedgehog foraging for food. By its size it wouldn't survive a winter of hibernation, so Katy decided to wrap it in her cardigan and take it home. I wanted to find a supply of slugs and moths, and let it fatten on them, but my wee sister said she'd rather look after the creature herself. That way she could keep an eye on it. Every winter she insisted on being a surrogate mother to some undernourished animal or bird. Mother, as usual, would be annoyed, but my sister took her stubborn streak from Dad, so into her cardigan went the prickly beastie.

After an hour or so, when we'd walked from our tent to the edge of the forest, we saw a woman. This was not unusual, apart from the fact she looked frightened; like she was being chased by something or someone. Her hair was all straggly, not brushed properly and tied up, just blowing wildly. Her clothes were tattered and torn, her eyes staring dead ahead.

I called out to see if she needed our help, but she kept on running, ignoring me. Katy saw that in the grass and brushwood a black cat was running at the woman's heel and called to it. The cat miaowed at us, then started off again behind the woman. I began running after them, but Katy said that if she ran her wee hedgehog would get shoogled up. So I took the beastie from the cardigan and put it inside my pocket. She sternly warned me not to run too fast, or else her pet would die for sure or get petrified with fright!

On and on went the woman, fleeing as if a demon from hell was on her heels, the cat behind her and us following. Suddenly, just as we were about to give up the chase, an inexplicable, extraordinary thing took place; the woman ran right through a tree, and just disappeared! We took one look at the tree, then at each other, before collapsing with fright.

Katy's bottom lip was trembling with the shock, when the cat came up and licked her hand. She stood up, and as she stooped to stroke the pussy it ran off towards our campsite. Our heads were still full of the vanishing lady, but we chased after the cat. When it got to the camp, it ran right through Granny's legs and into our tent.

Katy was clapping her hands and screaming, and it was just as well I'd got the wee hedgie in my pocket! Granny awakened with a jolt, nearly swallowing the clay pipe that she had lodged between her bottom teeth. When she saw how upset and terrified we were, she thought that someone was chasing us. She leaned down and grabbed hold of a thick tree branch.

We assured her there was no one there. I knew she'd not believe our mad woman story, but when Katy said a cat had gone into the tent, Granny's face lost every bit of its colour. The stick dropped from her fingers, and she began packing her belongings into the cart, murmuring in a strange tongue, and barking orders that we should pack up too. When I reminded her that Mother and Father would soon be home, tired and hungry, she seemed not to care, and said we'd meet them on the road. Within an hour the tent, with no sign of the cat, was down and folded. Baskets, pots, pans and all our worldly goods were neatly piled into our two-wheeled cart and the donkey yoked up.

Katy, although in a state of shock, said we had to feed the hedgehog and find it a home. No matter what, her wee beastie had to be cared for. Granny had previously made a pot of stew. With a ladle, she plopped some into a small dish. And while Katy sought out a deep hole under a nearby tree, the wee prickly scoffed every last drop. Then, totally unperturbed by events, it quite happily waddled inside the hole and curled up. Only then did Katy take Granny's hand as we walked out of the wood.

About a mile up the road we met mother and father. They were very angry and shouted at Granny, but when she told them an 'omen' had entered the tent, they understood and resigned themselves to finding another campsite, even though night was almost upon us. Kincladdie Wood at the other end of Dunning was a favoured spot, so we made for there. By the time we'd set up tent, lit a fire and reheated the stew, our eyes were heavy and bodies bone-tired.

I was last into bed, so it was my job to douse the fire and close the tent door. As I did so, a strange glow in the sky frightened me. I called for my family to come and see. Father said it looked like a fire, and a big one at that. Mother said she was so tired the sun could have fallen from heaven and it wouldn't make the slightest difference to her. I sat up for ages watching the orange phenomenon until the want of sleep sent me off to bed too.

Early next morning, after Mother and Father left for work, me and Katy washed our faces in a nearby burn, said cheerio to Granny and set off to play. As we explored our new play area, we heard Father calling. He had been looking for us. On their way to the farm our parents had met old Rab, the shepherd. This elderly man had been up all night with everyone from the village and the surrounding houses, putting out a haystack fire! The burning haystack, according to Rab, was right next to our previous campsite. Everybody thought that our tent had caught fire and that we must all have perished. When old Rab saw us coming along the road he was so happy he wanted us to go up with Granny to celebrate at the farm.

Many people came to see us, including the Provost of Dunning, who wanted to tell us how relieved he was that no one had perished in the flames. Granny told him and a stunned audience that it was Maggie Walls, a woman once famous as a witch, who had come and warned us of danger by leaving her cat as an omen.

Folks who lived round there knew full well that when Maggie was burned as a witch, although everybody searched for her cat, it was never found. Her cat is still her guardian. We Travellers know from ancestor stories that Maggie was a simple Tinker herb-woman who had never hurt a soul. Folk had got all excited in those olden days with an extreme type of religion, and were burning lots of people who knew only the ways of Mother Earth and not the teachings of the 'good book'.

Granny herself was a wise old woman, and if she'd been around in those days would probably have shared Maggie's fiery end!

Back at the camp, Katy was devouring her third jam-filled

scone, when she looked at me and then ran off towards the old camp ground. She was shouting as I chased after her that Hedgie had been left behind near where our tent had been, and she had to find out if the wee animal had perished in the fire.

What a shock we had when we came to the burnt ground, which was still smouldering. We both ran and started digging at the tree roots where Hedgie had been deposited. For a moment Katy froze in fear at what state he might be in, but as she gently felt inside the hole beneath the roots it was obvious from his curled body and shallow breathing that he was already sleeping for the winter.

Many times after that year we winter-stopped in Kincladdie Wood. Katy continued to watch out for injured animals, helping them when she could. When she grew up she moved far away to Canada. Granny lived until the ripe old age of 101. Our parents died in their fifties.

When I grew up and got married, my wife and I had three children. We lived in a house, where in the evenings we'd switch off the telly and by candlelight I'd tell my children stories of our times on the road. Their favourite tale was about Maggie Walls and her cat!

2

LUNARIA

This next tale is one that never fails to remind me that what seems perfectly delightful might not be quite as wonderful as it looks. A rich gentleman dreams of a beautiful wife. Does he find her?

The master, the Right Honourable Randolph Dollerie, stood outside his sprawling mansion surveying the marvel of granite excellence he'd had built for his pleasure. Every window was adorned with plush velvet curtains, and inside there was mahogany furniture from the Orient, the finest leather sofas and, as far as the eye could see, the plushest of wool carpets filled every inch of flooring. His bedchamber had all a gentleman of his status needed. There was a butler to attend to visitors; cooks to prepare food for the many dinner parties that he threw; there were horsemen, stable hands, chambermaids and many more, employed within stately Friarton Manor.

His father had built a coffee empire abroad, and by the time his young son had reached nineteen he'd inherited the entire fortune, which was considerable.

So there he stood, under a perfect full moon in the clearest of night skies, as friends and dignitaries made their way home and the staff bedded down for the night. It was such a lovely evening, so before going to bed, he thought he'd take a gentle meander through the forest.

Owls hooted when he entered the woods, and bats flew erratically at the sound of his boots crunching on a carpet of autumn leaves. Apart from those natural sounds, everything was still and quiet. As he walked, the conversation he'd had an hour earlier with his friends, while sipping brandy, came to mind and disturbed his peaceful stroll.

'Randolph, you must be about thirty, surely it's time you chose a wife?' asked Doctor Menzies, a close friend and confidant. 'I mean there's no shortage of beauties to choose from, and we can have another ball and invite debutantes from the continent.'

Lawyer Roberts added weight to the good doctor's proposal, saying, 'My sister Annabelle has two daughters ready for marriage. Quite lovely they are too, if you don't mind me saying so.'

Several others of his party guests who had his future at heart were all of the same opinion: it was time Randolph had a wife. After all, who would be his heir otherwise?

What they failed to grasp was that he'd not met anyone to love, and according to the natural law of life, surely this has a lot to do with finding a wife? To date he'd not met the right person. In fact the truth was that he'd not yet met the woman who came to him nightly in his dreams; she of sea-green eyes, jet-black hair, perfect form and peach-blushed skin. Randolph had lived a perfect life; he desired a perfect wife. But as 'she' was not a person of flesh and blood, only a simple figment of a lonely man's imagination, that's all she could be and, as he grew older, would remain.

Suddenly his path came to an end as a shimmering sheet of water appeared before him. The moon's light was shining upon the small loch at the forest edge. He'd not meant to walk such a distance, but lost as he was in his thoughts, he had misjudged the pathway. It had petered out and his footsteps now crunched on leaves.

But he wasn't tired, and it had been a long time since he had visited the picturesque scene. Moonbeams danced on the still water like gossamer fairies, and there was twinkling upon the black surface as if the stars had come down from the heavens to share the night. He sat down not caring if the ground was damp or not. He lay back and stared upwards, so grateful that he had decided to take a midnight stroll during a full moon.

'Hello.' The voice of a female came out of nowhere, utterly shattering his peace. He sat upright and looked around.

'I'm over here, by the laburnum tree. Stand up and you will see me,' the person said, in answer to his thoughts.

He stood up, then accidentally stumbled over a branch. A slender white arm reached over to steady him, and he stared into the most beautiful green eyes he'd ever seen.

'Where did you come from?' he asked, then wished he'd bitten off his tongue. He should have introduced himself first, as gentlemen are expected to do.

'You brought me here, did you not?'

'What kind of remark is that? Excuse me, my lady, but I have never set eyes on you before.'

Then, as she moved closer, he saw the face of his dreams.

'Yes, you have, my love.'

'What form of trickery is this?' He was shaking, unable to grasp that this was reality. 'I'm dreaming, aren't I?' he said, closing his eyes. Then two soft, ruby-red lips met his to prove that this was not a dream.

'Randolph, I am Lunaria, yours to keep and cherish for ever. From your desires I have come. It took many long, dark nights travelling through a maze of dreams to reach you, but with a totally committed love, I am here at last to share your life.' She touched his head, smiled sweetly and said, 'Shall we go home, my precious?'

They walked back in a magical state, his eyes drifting from the leafy path beneath their feet to her face of perfection. At last the turrets of Friarton Manor loomed on the horizon. When inside, under the chandeliers of the ballroom, he saw just how beautiful Lunaria really was. Of course she'd no clothes on, so he covered her with his cloak, then called on Charles, his butler, to make up a guest bedroom. His new-found vision of loveliness wouldn't hear of it, however, and insisted she sleep in his bedroom. Charles couldn't take in what was going on; first because he was half asleep, and secondly, her vivid beauty seemed to hold him spellbound, as it did the master.

That night Lunaria became Randolph's wife. There was no ceremony, no white dress or handmaidens, flowers or church bells. He had imagined her into existence, therefore she was his.

Next day it was clear to see that the master was under this charismatic lady's spell. She wasted no time in lining up all the household staff and instructing her husband to dismiss them. Without question he obeyed. From that moment it would be her responsibility to take care of the house and her darling husband. Within a week the entire household had packed up and left.

Lunaria adored horses, so she kept on stable boy Billy and Garrow the blacksmith. Apart from them, the place was left deserted.

She was everything Randolph had ever wanted or needed in a companion. In fact her attentiveness, at times, though welcome, was smothering. He certainly didn't miss his loyal staff, because she did all the cooking, cleaning, and household duties without the slightest problem. Flowers filled every room. Brightness and love abounded. And on the night of a full moon, she showered him with kindness and her undivided attention.

The first thing she did on these nights was to cut his nails and hair, fill a deep bath and add droplets of essential oils to relax him, and lastly gave him a small glass of her specially prepared wine. She said it was to celebrate their full moon anniversary. So much adoration mystified him, especially when she insisted sweeping his hair and nail cuttings into a stone jar and keeping them by her bed.

When word reached Randolph's friends about the mistress of Friarton, they simply had to visit – wild horses wouldn't have stopped them. When the vision of perfect beauty, wearing a blood-red, off-the-shoulder velvet gown, welcomed them with open arms, all curiosity was satisfied.

'She is the most delightful of creatures,' said Doctor Menzies, sounding like an excited little boy.

'Wherever did you find her?' asked Roberts, the lawyer. 'What a dark horse you turned out to be, keeping her a secret!'

Questions, some light, others probing deeper, came thick and fast, but Randolph told them nothing while his lovely wife stood by his side, smiling. Who would believe him, anyway? The truth was far too outrageous, and they would no doubt have sent him to an asylum if it had been revealed. This woman of his dreams had been a product of his success; she was nothing more or less than perfection, like all of his life.

Leaving him in peace with his new wife, his friends didn't visit as regularly as they had done previously, allowing Lunaria to have complete control over her husband. Strangely, he had been feeling under the weather recently, but didn't know why.

As day followed day, his strength began to fade. He no longer wished to go riding across his moorland with Lunaria on their favourite horses, or picnicking by the loch. Days passed painfully slowly, and as each went by his bones grew more stiff and sore. She insisted that soon the sickness would pass and he'd find new health. She put it down to nothing more than a virus.

He was never usually ill, and against her wishes, he visited his friend, the doctor, who after a thorough examination told him that he must have been doing too much work or something trivial. He must take lots of fresh air and a proper diet, and his health should improve.

It was a full moon again. Randolph had a dreadfully painful toothache, and didn't have the heart to say so, because his lovely wife was, as always, upbeat and happy and had spent the day pampering and preparing him for his rest. Trimmed nail cuttings along with hair snippings were put into the jar by the bed.

His soothing bath did nothing to help, and by the time both were in bed, the excruciating pain of toothache kept him wide awake.

As he lay there in the dark, he felt Lunaria rise from the bed, and heard her pulling something from underneath it. Then, after a few silent seconds, he felt a loop of leather slip around his neck; he knew from the feel of it that it was horse leather, but before words came to his lips the most unimaginable thing happened.

He was standing on the bedroom floor, not on two legs but four. He was a horse, a great big, strong, long-legged horse, saddled and bridled. 'I am dreaming, surely?' he thought, as he felt a leg swing over his back. Then, as if by magic, the wall opened and he was trotted out.

Out and upwards, he was being ridden into the night sky. The full glare of the moon blinded him as on he went, with the rider, whoever it was, on his back, guiding him. The rider certainly knew where to go. On and on they went, until he saw, far below, a great flaming fire.

Then a familiar voice whispered in his ear: 'Soon, my husband, soon you will be ours and your pain shall end.' It was Lunaria. The next sound tore through him – a screech-ing cackle of some old hag, definitely not his lovely wife.

Down they plummeted, to land upon a black rock where the fire raged. As he watched, unable to speak, he saw ap-proaching them hump-backed hags of the most fiendish appearance. They were witches in black hoods with pointed chins and hooked noses, pawing at his rider who was the ugliest hag of them all. He could hardly believe it when one said, 'Sister Lunaria, how fares your prey?'

Then, when the answer came, it left him in no doubt that he was wide awake, and that Lunaria, his vision of beauty, was a trickster of the most evil kind. 'He is near his end. One more lunar cycle and he will be ours!'

Randolph watched a scene of utter horror unfold before his eyes. Lunaria was completely unaware that he was not still spellbound. One by one the witches took stone jars from their belts. She, however, held hers tightly.

The female demons ran in unison, and threw the contents of their small stone jars into a giant one that was sitting on the fire. Instantly, as the nail and hair cuttings fell into the container, a scream of pain rent the air. It tore into Randolph's ears, piercing his very soul.

When the ceremony had finished and the cackling quietened, Lunaria leapt back into the saddle. She took to the air again, waving to her sisters from hell with promises that the next visit would be her victim's last – that victim being Randolph himself.

In no time he was lying on his bed, the halter removed, no longer a horse, but still with toothache and a deep determination to stop Lunaria from carrying out her deadly plan for his destruction.

He pretended not to know anything of what had happened, and hoped that this fiendish hag, disguised as a perfect woman, would not detect that his love had died. It was important, however, to pretend that he still felt the same. This was difficult to do, when he kissed her cheek, knowing what she really looked like.

Next day, although weaker than ever, he excused himself, saying he intended to visit his friend the doctor for removal of his tooth. She didn't suspect anything, and waved him off. The journey, although short, was hard because of his failing health, and he knew that by the next full moon he'd be so sick he'd not have any energy left.

'My friend,' he told the doctor, 'you can see that my strength is rather weaker than when last we met.'

'Yes, I must admit there is a significant change. Perhaps you should spend a few days in bed. I will give Lunaria a bottle of medicine to administer to you.'

'You will do no such thing. She is behind my ill health. It is a fiendish devil I am married to, a demon from hell!' Randolph had no intention of disclosing his plans to the Doctor, but hearing the mention of her name sent him into a fit of temper.

'This illness of yours has made you delusional. Your lovely wife is nothing less than a saint, running the house single-handedly, tending your needs! No, I think you should take full bed-rest, my friend. I shall visit you every week until you're on your feet again.'

Randolph had a plan in mind, but it seemed that his friend was as much under Lunaria's spell as he once had been. Proof was needed. On the eve of the next full moon, he instructed Billy, his faithful stablehand, to have his friends waiting in the courtyard, early the next morning. He then asked Garrow, the blacksmith, to forge two extremely heavy horseshoes and await his instructions. He had to be in the courtyard too.

The cycle of the moon came round again. The ritual of the day once over, he again found himself lying in bed, but this time things would be different. He heard Lunaria rise as before, pulling the box out from beneath the bed and taking out the halter. But the moment it touched his head, he turned around, grabbed it from her and slipped it over her head instead. Instantly she was a grey mare, eyes rolling in her equine head, neighing loudly.

Randolph looped a leather strap around her mouth, stopping her from making any sound, and pulled himself onto her back. Her journey was mapped before them: out through the bedroom wall, up into the night sky, flitting across the rays of moonlight, heading onwards to find her home of flame, with her witch sisters and their soul jars. In seconds, down she plummeted, to land in exactly the same spot as before. Randolph had wrapped a long hooded cloak around himself; he needed a disguise to trick the others. The only problem was, he'd very little energy left.

'Hello, Lunaria, sister of the moon,' said one ghoul,

creeping over to him. 'This night you have brought the young master of Friarton Manor to join the others?'

He nodded. Holding up the small stone jar and keeping his head down, he strode over to the waiting flames. He threw his small one into the giant jar, but nothing happened. A low growl and then a shrill squealing rent the night air, as one by one the demons realised their sister was too quiet and this cloaked creature was far too tall.

He took from under his cloak a heavy wood stake, and before the witches could reach him, hit the giant jar so hard it split into a dozen pieces, sending every witch into a fit of frenzied screaming. 'Eek, we've lost the souls! Catch them, Catch them! Eek! Eek!'

Round and round they flew, on batlike wings, trying to halt the stream of misty souls who were escaping towards their heavenly home. There were many men, obviously sad departed victims of the other witches. They waved and smiled as they went, watching him as he ran over to climb on the back of Lunaria and make his escape. The next moment the earth split open and swallowed up all the witches, the broken jar and the flames.

A few minutes later, he was still clinging desperately to his horse's neck as she landed in the courtyard.

Rushing past his opened-mouthed friends, he called on Garrow to bring the horseshoes. Telling everyone to stay away from the grey mare, he held her close, keeping an extra tight hold on the halter round her neck. 'This fine horse is my beautiful wife. A woman who is married to the devil, and plots my destruction!'

'What madness is this?' said Menzies.

Roberts shook his head, and said that their dear friend Randolph was mad and should be locked up.

'Shoe the mare's front hooves,' he shouted to Garrow, ignoring everyone else, 'make them fit.'

Garrow expertly shoed the mare, then stood clear as his employer instructed.

'Now you shall all see why my health is failing me. See what I have been living with!' He slipped off the leather halter, and in an instant, there, for all eyes to see, stood an old wizened hag, cackling loudly. Pointed chin almost touching her hooked nose, she screeched that she was a sister of the Luna spirit – a witch of the moon! 'No one can stop me from departing this place. I will find more fools to romance; my power is greater than that of mere mortals.'

She lifted her head to meet the first rays of sunshine, laughed, let out an unearthly squeal and tried to fly off – but she'd forgotten that the earth has a magic of her own. The iron shoes and nails held her and bound her feet to the ground. She tried desperately to free herself, but the shoes were far too heavy, she was going nowhere.

'I need a pit of lime to burn her in. Who will help me?' Randolph asked. He did not have to ask twice, because in no time his friends, equipped with spades, dug a large pit half filled with lime. They threw her in, still screaming defiance, and when the lime had reduced her to ashes, they filled the hole with more lime and soil. Lunaria would never again trick any man.

From then on Randolph, whose health soon returned to normal, filled Friarton Manor with a busy household of butler, cooks, chambermaids and countless others. He never married. People say that on the night of a full moon, he refused to go to bed and spent the whole night sitting by the main window of the house, simply staring out into the darkness.

3

CLACH MOR

If I have a really busy day ahead telling stories, I sometimes begin with a bowl of porridge or a big glass of mixed fruit, crushed pineapple, banana and apple, swirled up with orange juice. Why don't you have a nice healthy smoothie while I tell you this old tale…?

I heard it for the first time near Kirkmicheal in Highland Perthshire. Clach Mor, the title of the story, is Gaelic for 'big stone'.

Having read the last two tales, I have a question for you – do you believe in witches? You do? Well, read on.

Tiptoe quietly into the world of a very evil ruler, the Wolf of Badenoch, and his partner in the underworld, An Chealach – a humpy-backed, sharp-nosed, beady-eyed old witch.

The Wolf of Badenoch was what the tortured people of Highland Scotland named him, and it was around the fourteenth century he ruled much of the area with an iron fist. Not one single good deed had he done in his entire life.

Children were banned from playing, young men were enslaved into his army on threat of beheading if they refused, women were ordered to stay indoors. His domain was a sad and desolate place, wherein he sat enthroned in a great castle named Cullic, surrounded by the black water of a forty-foot wide moat.

No one challenged him or dared to end his tyranny, because folk swore that he was too powerful. Not only that, but it was believed he had the power of a devil, and many a night, strange and eerie sounds were heard coming from the castle dungeons. Terrified mothers locked up their daughters in fear of them disappearing in the dead of night, to end up as sacrifices to ghouls and demons.

Thankfully, on one night of thunder and lightning, old age brought his days to an end. He'd breathed his last. A secret funeral was attended by his son and heir, and also his faithful companion – An Chealach, the witch.

Next day, when news of his passing circulated throughout the area, people celebrated in music and song. Parties went on for days, because at long last their suffering was over. Now children could play in peace, young woman walk to market without fear of being kidnapped, and all would once more be as quiet and peaceful as it had been before Badenoch ruled.

There was one question on everyone's lips: 'Will his son, the young Badenoch, be more of a tyrant than his father?'

Locals spoke of little else, but said to each other, 'Nobody could possibly be as evil.' They began to feel more relaxed in their everyday lives and to forget the shadow of evil that hung around Cullic Castle.

All their hopes and joys were dashed, however, when it emerged that the young Wolf was in fact worse – much worse!

It was a stormy night when orders came forth that summoned all of Badenoch's builders to the great hall of the castle. Their master desired of them a monumental task.

'I wish that the castle, this ugly, old, crumbling ruin, be brought down and another built in its place!'

'Master,' an old builder dared to say, 'this is a sturdy building with plenty of heart left in it. Surely, for your pleasure, we could improve its battlements and add a dungeon or two?'

'I will not allow you to comment on my desire to rid the land of this monstrosity. It may have suited my late father, but not me!' He lowered himself into his new throne, threw back his cloak of ermine and purple silk, leant his chin on his hand and said, 'The Clach Dubh Mor of Ballachullish is my preferred stone for building the new castle. Any enemy that attempts to scale its height will slide down and be swallowed by the murky swamp below. Furthermore, the height of the castle shall touch the very clouds that fill the sky! Now, be off to plan my stronghold. At once, I command you!'

The unfortunate builder who had spoken against the plan was already being dragged away to feel the point of a sharp sword. The master builder, although in fear of his own life, stepped forward and tried to reason with his master. 'Sire, it would be foolish to rid the land of her finest builders. Surely you would be wise to listen to our wisdom in this matter.'

Badenoch sat back and for a while mulled over the man's words. He wasn't just any builder; indeed he had held the highest reputation for creating the old ruler's constructions.

'Speak,' he ordered.

'Sire, we commend you for embarking on such grand projects, but the Clach Mor of Ballachullish is slate. It crumbles at the slightest touch. Yes, we could build you a new castle of solid granite, the finest in all the land, and adorn the roof with the slate of the Clach Mor, but that is all. And even if the stone was suitable for building, transporting it fifty miles from the west could not be undertaken. What you ask is impossible.'

Badenoch grew angrier and screeched at the top of his voice. Terrified builders fell over each other in the rush to escape from the hall as his booming voice echoed from wall to wall.

Alone with his darkening mood and simmering anger, he reflected that, when men were no use to his father, he sought out the help of another power. Old Nick, the Devil himself, would not refuse him.

Pulling his cloak around his shoulders, he rushed off. Soon his footsteps echoed loudly downwards into the depths of the castle dungeons.

'Master of darkness, keeper of evil, 'tis I, son of Badenoch. The young Wolf calls on you. Come to me, I command!'

Mist and ghostly shadows listened to the hollow echoes of his voice inside the dungeon, but no sound came from the black oak door of the room where the lord of darkness had, not that long ago, supped whisky and played cards with his old father. The sacrificial table where the killing of young, innocent damsels had been carried out stood desolate and marble cold. In his anger and sorely-tried frustration Badenoch thumped it, and shouted, 'Now, I say, at once, meet me for discussions! I need my Clach Dubh Mor castle, and I want it now!'

Raising his voice to an almighty screech, he demanded an audience with the devil, but still no sound or movement occurred. Chill winds sent a shiver down his spine and his patience wore paper thin. For at least an hour he waited and waited; but nothing, not even so much as a black moth, moved in the deathly chamber.

'Am I to be denied the help of all men and devils, this wretched night?'

He had no more patience left, so turning on his heel with a swish of his flowing cloak, he hurried out of the dark room. As he was departing a sudden movement in a recess halted him. 'Who hides like a cowed dog in my castle?' he called into the darkness.

'I, only I, sire.'

'And who, may I ask, are you?'

'An Chealach. Your obedient servant.'

'Ach, foolish old woman, begone to your bed and leave me.'

'Master, if it be your pleasure I can help.'

'What can the likes of a bent, twisted, pointed-chinned hag do for me?'

'I overheard the conversation with your builders, and may I say, sire, begging your pardon, but I know how to dislodge the Clach Dubh Mor of Ballachullish.'

He stopped and turned towards her. 'Speak, or see your tongue be parted from your miserable wretched throat.'

'Follow me. I live down here, and in my chambers I have something you need to see.'

Badenoch felt drawn in a strange way towards the witch, but then she had a way of casting spells. In this knowledge he stopped, and said angrily, 'My mood darkens with the night, so this had better be good!'

After a short walk, she beckoned him under an archway of stone and into a small room. It was dark and dingy, smelling of dust and mould. He refused her offer of a chair.

'How, old hag, can you get stones for my castle?'

'Sit down, young master, and I shall first tell you a story. Then we shall see.'

She pointed once more to the seat, but still he refused to take it. Seeing his reluctance, she asked instead if he would please glance into a pot of boiling liquid bubbling on a stove in the room. This he did, and as he looked inside she stood beside him, both gazing down at the contents of the pot. What he saw sent a shiver down his spine, he almost fell backwards in shock. 'Who is she?' he asked.

He held the old woman tightly by the shoulders, demanding to know who the beautiful girl was who was staring out at him from the depth of the soup.

'As I said, master, sit down while I tell you a story.'

He slumped into the chair, resting his hands on its two wooden arms, head filled with the vision from within the soup pot.

'Once,' she began, 'there was a beautiful girl who belonged to the Lord of Darkness. He had for some time been listening to the wife of a church minister praying to him. At night, when her husband left to conduct a service for his parishioners, she would lie upon the floor and call for my master to give her eternal youth. The beautiful girl you have just seen was sent to the minister's wife to bring her down here, where the master would grant the woman's wish: eternal youth in exchange for her soul.

The minister's wife asked the girl what payment she wanted, but her master had strictly instructed the girl not to accept gifts. Against his orders, the girl took the woman's apron as a gift. When the Devil heard of this, he instantly stripped away the girl's beauty, turning her into a horrible, ugly witch. I am that girl, and the image you have seen was me.'

'But this is a tragedy – you wither away down here when you could share my home, be my wife. I shall ask the master to give you back your beauty, at once.'

She lifted her head and cackled loudly, sending hanging bats flying erratically up and down the corridors. 'No man, no matter how powerful, can tell the King of Darkness what to do. He could turn you into a frog and crush the very life from your body, without so much as rising from his seat. But listen to me, my handsome young love, for ages I have crept into your room while you slept and watched over you. While out hunting in the woods, do you remember when the black stallion threw you? Well, who do you think saved you? You can't remember, because of the head injuries you suffered. My dear young Wolf, I love you more than any woman can.' She touched his arm with her long bony fingers, but he did not push her away, because soon, if all went to plan, the slender, soft hand of the beautiful young girl would replace them, and he and she would be man and wife.

Now that she had ensnared him, she eagerly moved closer to him. 'Here is my plan. This very night, as the moon fulls in the sky, you must take several soldiers and ride out of the castle. Break down doors and steal seven children. Bring them here and give each one as a sacrifice to my master. Call on him quietly, bowing as you do so. Remember, no mortal comes without gifts. Ask him for only one thing – my beauty. As for the stone of Ballachullish, with my magic apron I shall see to that. This time tomorrow you shall have your castle, and I shall once more be beautiful.'

His eyes widened with excitement, and for a moment forgetting how ugly and grotesque his companion was, he drew her close and kissed her cold grey cheek. She let out a yell of delight, and while he dashed off to give orders and saddle his horse, she was already sitting astride her broomstick, heading westwards to gather the precious stone.

Now, if any living beings were near that dreaded place

you would think that they could be only creatures of the night – goblins and ghouls. However the Good Witch of All Things Pure knew that, as far as An Cealach was concerned, a 24-hour watch was essential. In two slit windows in the dungeon wall sat a pair of her helpers, tiny fairies known as Sithein. They had listened intently to the conversation between the young Wolf and the old witch.

On gossamer wings the tiny fairies flew as fast as they could to tell the Good Witch what was about to happen.

'Oh my dears, of all the most awful things that evil has a hand in, this must be the worst!' cried the Good Witch. 'We have very little time, because when An Cealach bestrides her broom of rowan, she speeds faster than sound.'

The Good Witch summoned a thousand of her helpers to take a single strand of lamb's wool and use it to cover the huge expanse of slate stone. Then she gathered another band of little people and gave a stern order. 'My children,' she said, 'each take a droplet of my special sleeping draught, put it on the lips of the Wolf's soldiers, and they will not awaken until morning. When you have finished with that task, tie their horses' tails together.'

Without a question the army of Sithein flew as one body into the sky, and like a giant dove headed westwards.

They arrived at the great stone without a moment to spare, and covered every inch of the Ballachullish slate with the lamb's wool. As the last strand was put in place, the dark-cloaked witch came and hovered above. Not seeing a single black stone beneath her, she found a crevice between some rocks and sat simmering in her rage. As she screeched and punched the air, a sister witch joined her to see what was wrong. 'Sithein, those horrid wee goblins, have tricked me – not a stone is anywhere to be seen.'

'What stones do you seek, my wretched kin?'

'Are ye blind as well as stupid? I seek the Ballachullish stone to build a castle.'

'Oh, is that all?'

'All! All! Look at me, am I not hideous? Badenoch is, at this moment, sacrificing seven children to our master. I promised him a castle of the slate stone, and then he would have my beauty restored and we shall be wed! Our double task must be completed before the full moon slips from the night sky. Aargh, I am in turmoil!'

Her sister coiled a bony arm around her shoulder and whispered, 'Listen, foolish hag, have you forgotten where we spend our Halloweens?'

'No, I have never missed one of our parties on the Isle of Man!'

'Well, is the Clach Dubh Mor not in abundance there?'

'Why, of course!' An Cealach kicked up her bandy legs and somersaulted five times, before curling her body round her broomstick like a skinny cobra. 'Mighty is the stone of black! Thank you, oh kind sister.' Instantly she was scooting across the moon in all its fullness, like a Daddy-long-legs being chased by a flying bat.

No sooner had she left the mountainous terrain of Scotland, than she was staring wide-eyed at an expanse of gleaming black stone beneath her – enough to build a dozen castles! It wasn't quite what her betrothed wished for, but this was better. He'd be well pleased when the final hellish stone was placed on his castle above the clouds themselves.

There was no time to lose. With her magic apron tied around the gigantic, smooth as silk stone she had chosen, she was already in flight, heading north, to begin a night-long task that would result in a magnificent castle for her lover and her youthful beauty restored.

Now, as fate would have it, an old poacher was out taking advantage of the full moon's light and was heading home, dead deer on his back. As An Chealach, with her precious cargo, blotted for an instant the light on his path, he looked up. When he saw the vision above him, he fell to his knees and said, 'God preserve us!' As his divine words flitted heavenwards, they passed through the witch's apron. Penetrated by such godly words, its power began to wane. Tumbling downwards went the giant stone, loosened from its sling. It spiralled down until it hit the ground with the most horrendous thump!

An Chealach screamed as she plummeted after it. Meanwhile young Badenoch, unable to rouse his men from their hypnotic slumber, ran back and forth roaring at the top of his voice for An Chealach. But, alas, the humpy-backit old witch was frantically digging around the base of the stone that had fallen, wailing and screaming as the moon dropped from the starry sky, giving way to the first rays of the sun.

The young Wolf who had planned to oversee his late father's powers of darkness and the building of a new black stone castle was to be seen many a night standing on the battlements of his crumbling fortress. He was gazing out into the darkness, waiting for his lost love who, like his dream of a new castle, had evaporated from the base of the big stone at the first touch of sunlight, like a swirl of steam from a slow-boiling kettle.

Fairy folk and the Good Witch from then on enjoyed the singing of young women, the playing of little children in sun-kissed meadows and the merry laughter of men who lived in harmony from that day to this, in the peaceful area of picturesque Badenoch.

Locals used to say that on Halloween, if they dared to go past the spot where the stone had fallen, An Cealach could be heard cursing the wee fairy folk who put paid to her dream of being the Wolf of Badenoch's beautiful queen.

4

JEANNIE'S GOLD

My mother was a wonderful storyteller, and some nights, especially long dark winter ones, she would tell us tales of kings and queens of history, and even of kings and queens that never were. This is one such tale…

Scottish history books tell the story of Flora Macdonald, and how she saved Bonnie Prince Charlie by dressing him up as her Irish maidservant, Betty Burke.

Bonnie Prince Charlie had come to Scotland in 1745 to take the throne of Britain from the reigning king, because he was convinced that his own family, the Stuarts, were the rightful rulers. The followers who flocked to meet him and fight in his army were called Jacobites. Historians tell of the Jacobites' final defeat at the Battle of Culloden. After the battle, Bonnie Prince Charlie was hurried off from the Culloden battlefield on the outskirts of Inverness, and smuggled onto the island of Uist. There he met Flora Macdonald. Next to tales of William Wallace and Robert the Bruce, the story of their journey of escape, from Benbecula on South Uist to Portree on Skye, is one of the most famous in Scottish history.

The chance that they might meet parties of Redcoats from the enemy army marauding throughout Skye put them in extreme danger. Their escape went smoothly in the end: the Betty Burke disguise certainly proved its worth in securing the safe departure of the country's would-be monarch. He sailed off and was swallowed up in a swirling mist, never to set foot on Scotland's shores again. Sad and dejected, he settled on the continent and thereafter lived out his life in obscurity.

Here is the story about these events that Mother told us. Are you sitting comfortably? Good. Then let's rewrite history, for our own enjoyment.

Jeannie Macarthur stood at her gate on the island of Uist, head covered by a shawl of greenish-grey, waiting and watching. Her brother Donald hadn't come home from the Battle of Culloden. News had trickled back to Uist that many had fallen. Defeat soon followed. People were dashing this way and that, like headless hens. The enemy were coming to burn and murder, according to the news carriers. The Duke of Cumberland, the leader of the Redcoats and second son of King George of England, had won – to him went the spoils.

Like red lines of adders, his bloodthirsty troops searched through every inch of Highland homes. Spirals of black smoke wound upwards to mingle with the fog that shrouded the sky. It was a time of terror, a time to run and hide. The cause of the Jacobites was lost forever. Culloden Moor was soaked in their blood, and the victorious Duke of Cumberland raised the flag of St George for all Highland eyes to see. Bonny Prince Charlie had stood his ground until the last clansman fell in his defence, before being smuggled away amidst weeping and wailing.

SOOKIN' BERRIES

Flora Macdonald, from Milton on South Uist, lived in Edinburgh, but was visiting her father on the island when these events took place. Suddenly a young boy rushed into the house. Her father, who was a tenant farmer, recognised Jamie Macdonald. 'What ails you, boy?' he asked, grabbing him by the shoulders to stop him shaking. 'What is wrong, son?' he asked again.

Without answering him, the lad rushed over to Flora and said, 'Mistress, your brother needs you right now!'

'My goodness,' she said, 'what a terrible state you're in. I'll get my cloak.'

In no time she was half-running and half-stumbling over runrigs, falling over rocks and finding it very hard to keep up with the wide-eyed, pale-faced boy. Soon they stood at her brother's low-roofed cottage, soaked through by a heavy shower of summer rain.

When she opened the door and stepped inside, her brother rushed over. 'Thank God, sister, you have come.'

'What is the matter?' she asked him. 'This youngster wouldn't tell me!'

'Come over and dry yourself at the fire, and meet our visitor.'

Flora darted her eyes around the corners of the small house, and from a shadowy recess a man stepped out who needed no introduction. In thick plaid of the finest Stewart tartan and a deep purple bonnet with a white cockade fixed among feathery plumage, stood the Jacobite monarch himself, Bonnie Prince Charlie.

Flora fell back into a small armchair, hardly able to breathe. When eventually she found her voice, she whispered to her brother, 'If the Redcoats know his whereabouts we shall all be put to the sword!'

'Look, Flora, this may sound like madness, but the only way we can save the Prince is to disguise him. Have you a spare dress?'

Her mouth dropped open at his suggestion. Panic-stricken and in fear that at any moment the enemy would burst in and kill them all, she answered, 'I stand here before you in the only dress I have. My wardrobe is in my house, and that, as you know is in Edinburgh. I don't even have a spare yard of tweed.'

The Prince, who had stayed silent until then, spoke quietly without the slightest sign of fear. 'Madam, a boat waits near Portree in Skye to carry me to France. Word is that if we can get there by the weekend, I shall be able to sail from Scotland. Cumberland will kill and murder until he finds me, so the quicker I leave the better for all. Please, milady, can you think of a way? So much depends on my departure.'

Flora could see the desperate state of affairs and thought hard. Suddenly an idea came to her. 'Wee Jeannie!' she shouted.

She called Jamie, who'd been sitting quietly on guard by the window. 'Go and fetch Jeannie Macarthur, the seam-stress. If anyone can conjure up a dress to fit the Prince then I know no other. Uist folk say she can sew the wings back onto a seagull. Tell her to fetch every spare piece of plaid she can find, and her sewing box.'

She was excited and frightened at the same time: it was such a fantastic idea, but if the Prince was to be saved, then this surely must be the way. 'Brother, strip your bed. If Jeannie can sew together the dress, then our prince must be disguised as my maidservant.'

In less than an hour, the young lad came panting back

into the house, Jeannie Macarthur at his back. She laid a bag of plaid cuttings on the floor, sat a rickety old box next to it and said, 'Well, Mistress Macdonald, this had better be important. I've left my poor mother standing at the end of our path. She's in an awful state because our Donald hasn't come home from the battle. I've heard tell the young Prince is hiding someplace in the great glen with nothing more than a couple of worthy men to save him, and Cumberland's butchers are trailing every inch of the Highlands and islands searching out Jacobites and running them through. Blood is soaking our land, so I've more to worry about than mending a frock! Now, what is it you want of me that has turned young Jamie near hairless?'

Softly, as the others looked on, Prince Charlie laid his hands on Jeannie's shoulders and turned her to face him. 'You, I'm informed, can sew the wings back onto a gull and let it fly off whole?' He stared into her eyes, and like Flora she knew immediately who he was. She fell hard on her knees as the sight of him sent shock-waves through her body. 'Well, I'd not go to that extent, your Royal Highness, but I'm a keen seamstress.'

'You're the best there is,' said Flora, helping her onto shaky legs. 'Now, Jeannie, what is needed – and remember time is not on our side – is a frock to fit the Prince. He will sail across to Skye with me disguised as Betty Burke, my maidservant from Ireland. We shall travel over Syke to Portree, where a boat waits to take him to France.'

Without a word, Jeannie began pulling strips of plaid from her rag bag. She pushed feet out of her way as she laid the strips side by side on the floor. Flora's brother laid sheets and blankets before her. Then, as if by magic, her fingers were sowing and cutting. On and on, as if in a trance, her little fingers jigged and jumped, scissors cut and tore. The onlookers were fascinated as the garment began to take shape.

One hour passed, then two, three and four, and by the sixth hour a dress lay on her lap. Sweat trickled from her brow. 'Here,' she said, handing the dress to the Prince, 'away you into the room and try that on!'

What an amazing transformation: gone was the man, and there for all eyes to marvel at was Betty Burke, Irish maidservant to Flora Macdonald.

'I'll challenge anyone to find the man in that woman,' laughed Jamie, before he left to head home. He'd no idea if his own father and brother, who had set off the previous month to take arms for the Jacobite cause, were alive or dead, but with the work complete, he'd a contented look on his face, knowing he had played his part. Prince Charlie thanked him warmly.

Flora's brother set four bowls on an old pine table, and ladled a helping of broth into each. The soup with some bread was shared between them. Flora and Charlie went over their stories if they should be stopped by Redcoats, before leaving to row across from Benbecula to Skye. Jeannie was already halfway down the sheep path leading from their house to hers when the Prince called her back. 'Jeannie,' he asked softly, trying to speak with a feminine tone, 'where are you going?'

'Home, Sire, to see if my mother is alright and to see if there's any news of my brother Donald,' she told him.

'Would you consider taking this journey with us? I think three women would fare better than two, don't you agree?'

For a moment she thought how helpless they looked, Flora with her Edinburgh-pale skin, and him – she couldn't at that moment make up her mind what he looked like – but he was right, another woman might be an advantage if they should catch the attention of enemy soldiers, especially if they'd been drinking.

'Skye, ye say? Well, after all I am the daughter of Donald John Macarthur, a true-blooded Jacobite, and even if he be dead in his grave, I know he'd not rest in peace if I did not see the prince of the line of the Stuarts to safety.'

'Even if you lose your life in the process?' asked Flora.

'My life is not important, and come to think of it, compared with seeing the Prince to safety, neither is my blessed mother. Can you tell her I'm away to help with the cause?'

She dropped her sewing box at the feet of Flora's brother, who nodded. Tying a coarse wool shawl around her shoulders, she linked arms and said, 'Come now, you two fine lassies, let's get ourselves over the sea to Skye.'

Thankfully, brisk winds filled the sails of the little boat, which allowed them to make speedy progress, and carried them from Benbecula on Uist to Skye in relative safety. It was 27 June 1746.

Night was falling as they waded onshore. Flora and Jeannie knew the paths well, having been many times on the island. Even with darkness engulfing them, they were able to push on with speed. At around four in the morning, the darkest hour, they found a rocky cleugh where they could curl up and rest. They'd brought dried strips of beef to eat, which were soon downed with a drink of fresh water from a small stream.

Halfway through the day, a frightening sound drifted from a small ring of thatched cottages nearby. It was a band of unruly Redcoats. They were armed with flaming torches and were about to set fire to the houses. With torches held high, they began shouting orders that all inhabitants had to flee or be burned inside. Horrified, the threesome saw women and children rushing around trying to salvage what little they could before the fire took hold.

'Help, help!' A young woman who was heavily pregnant ran to one of the Redcoats. 'My little girl is still in her bed, she has a fever – please get her out!'

An officer pushed her roughly aside, ignoring her pleas. 'She can burn among all the rest of the rubbish,' he snarled like a dog. He spat at her feet and stiffly strode off.

Jeannie couldn't stand by and watch. Picking up her skirt she ran as fast as her legs would carry her. Ignoring the enemy soldiers, she rushed through them and into the house. Flames roared round her among black smoke; inside the heat and fumes were unbearable as she felt blindly for a bed. At first she thought her lungs might give in, when a tiny hand found hers. In seconds she had the child, face blackened with smoke, resting, barely alive, in the arms of her grateful mother.

A soldier stormed over and slapped her hard across the face. 'I've a good mind to throw you into the flames,' he yelled as she lay on the ground. An old woman threw herself onto Jeannie's body and took the full force of a powerful kick aimed for her. She gave a painful sigh and rolled over, eyes flickering in her time-ravaged face. Jeannie, ignoring the onslaught of abuse from her tormentor, held the old woman until she breathed her last, then screamed, 'You evil pig! You've killed her.'

The officer, who obviously had a busy day ahead, smartly intervened and ordered his soldiers away. The days that followed for the Highlands and islands were as dark and blood-spattered as any in their history.

SOOKIN' BERRIES

After the soldiers had gone, Flora scolded Jeannie and said, 'Are you forgetting whose life is at stake?' She pointed to the Prince who was sadly watching the line of broken families wending their way over the old drove road. He told Jeannie that she had been very brave, and then he said something that astonished both women. 'As I'm to blame for all this, is there time to bury the old woman?'

Flora, only 21 years old, was already taking control, and showing the wisdom of a woman twice her age. 'No, Sire, not a minute can we spare. But she lived the hard life, and will be content to know her thin frame shall feed the crows and the gulls. God will catch her soul!'

The battle on Culloden Moor had reduced the Prince to a poor wretched creature. He slumped down and dropped his head. 'What has been done in my name is too awful to contend with,' he said. Aware of the sacrifices that had been made throughout the land for the Stuart cause, he cried, 'Madam, I am a total failure and do not deserve to live, but allow me to complete one task.' He stood up and went down to where the still form of the dead woman lay.

'At least let me drape her body with bracken!' he said. Jeannie and Flora dashed around pulling clumps of heather and handfuls of bright green fern, and in less than five minutes they had completely covered the body. After saying a few prayers in Latin, they were soon striding onwards. As the clock ticked on, no one, friend or foe, barred their path.

That night it was decided each should take a turn guarding the others as they slept, and by early morning they had replenished their energies. After more strips of cold beef and fresh water, they were once again on their treacherous road. All that day went by without incident, and they had another night of relative peace.

Next morning, as they washed at the burn, Jeannie noticed Charlie's chin. It was a real giveaway – his beard was well sprouted. This posed a big problem, for they had no razor, nor any other way of removing the offending growth. Both women advised him to cover the lower part of his face, which he did.

It was Sunday, and the final stretch lay ahead. Each prayed that the cruel Redcoats would keep clear, as every step brought them nearer to Portree where a sturdy boat waited for Charlie. With the town in their sights, and only another mile to go, a sound made their hearts stop. Drums were beating loudly from within the scattered thatched cottages of the Braes, followed by spirals of thick black smoke. They halted in their tracks.

As if by magic, a wave of Redcoats descended on them, brandishing rifles with fixed bayonets. By the look and the noise of them, it was easy to tell that a night of drinking and pillaging had just taken place.

Flora froze, then she reached down to grab the Prince's hand and squeezed it tight. Quickly he covered a now healthy red beard with the shawl. They were in full view of the drunken soldiers, who wasted no time in circling them. Flora's heart was beating louder than the drumbeats booming from around the burning houses. 'This is the end,' she thought, as one man reached up to pull the shawl from Charlie's head.

Jeannie had other ideas, and wasn't giving up, after travelling all that way, without a fight. As hard as she could bear, she bit down on her tongue. Blood oozed and trickled profusely from each corner of her mouth. The Redcoats saw her, and now she had their attention she threw herself on the ground and arched her spine. With the blood oozing and back curved, she made sounds that could only be described as terrifying. She was gargling, groaning and frothing. Flora dashed forward, saying, 'She has the sickness! Don't touch her, flee for your lives!'

If the soldiers had been sober, then perhaps Jeannie's play-acting wouldn't have had the same effect, but in their intoxicated state, each one feared catching the dreaded disease, whatever it was, and took to their heels.

Flora helped Jeannie to her feet, and with skirts at knee level the small band ran as fast as their legs could carry them. Not once did they stop to look back, until, almost breathless, they stood on the shore at Portree.

Out to sea, waiting in silence, stood the ship ready to ferry Charlie away. A small rowing boat, with one solitary oarsman, rolled from side to side on the incoming tide.

Charlie removed his Betty Burke disguise and hastily dressed in his own clothes, while Jeannie and Flora grew sadder by the minute.

'Madam,' he said to Flora, 'perhaps one day we may meet again. I will think of you every day of my life and of what might have been. The clans will never be reunited; Culloden and King George have seen to that. Cumberland, his butcher of a son, has only just begun his march of death. I am profoundly sorry that my time in Scotland has been so short. I shall go back to France and write letters to all Europe to save Scotland from the impending reign of the sword, this I promise you.'

He went onto one knee and kissed her small hand, pressing into it a gold locket containing his portrait. Turning to Jeannie, he said, 'Ah, my little heroine, the bravery I have witnessed this day gives me hope that if all Scotland's mothers and daughters have your strength, then she will survive without any monarch at her helm. I want to give you so much, but alas I have only one thing.' He reached into a small pocket in his tunic and retrieved a gold coin. Gently he took her trembling hand and laid it on her palm. 'Take this, Jeannie Macarthur. It is the gold of Scotland and I give it to you!'

Opening his arms, he beckoned them both to him, and for a few moments they held each other until the impatient oarsman reminded him of the Redcoats nearby.

Jeannie and Flora watched as the waves carried their king who never was away. Through the sea mist he could just be seen climbing aboard the sailing vessel, and then he was gone. They would never see him again.

Word of their escapade and the part they played in it reached enemy ears. Flora was arrested two weeks later, and taken from her father's home to be imprisoned in Dunstaffnage Castle, before being sent to the Tower of London. She was released in 1747 under a general amnesty which freed many of those who had fought against the government. (Prince Charlie had promised to write letters to every ruler in Europe, and perhaps it was his efforts that brought about this turn of events.)

Flora married a Uist man named Alan MacDonald and then emigrated to North Carolina. Her husband joined a regiment of Royal Highland Emigrants, and took part in the American War of Independence. He was captured at the battle of Moore's Creek and for a time was imprisoned before being sent to Nova Scotia. In 1779 the couple returned to Skye where they lived out their lives. Flora died in Kingsburgh in the same bed in which Bonnie Prince Charlie had slept during his short attempt to unite the clans and give Scotland a king.

SOOKIN' BERRIES

Jeannie Macarthur went home to find that Donald had come home, battle-weary but safe. She decided to enter a nunnery and devote her life to tending the poor and infirm. To Donald she gave the 'Prince's coin', making him solemnly swear to hand it down through the Macarthur line. This he did. His son Alexander inherited the precious relic; he in turn passed it to his daughter Elizabeth, who passed it to her son Alexander, who passed it to his daughter Margaret, who passed it to her daughter Jeannie, who passed it to her daughter Jess (me!).

I have taken the coin to many storytelling events, and my listeners just have to feel the old relic to know it carries a tale. It is a coin from between 1690 and 1730. Now, because of its worn state, I am forced to keep it in a glass box, where after hearing its story all can view its beauty.

5

THE ROBIN'S CHRISTMAS SONG

Let us enjoy a bit of old Scottish dialect with this wonderful tale by Scotland's national bard, Robert Burns. I am going to use his original Scots in the telling of it. Then I shall copy it into English, so that all readers can understand and enjoy Robbie's story.

Robbie Burns was a poet rather than a storyteller, but that didn't mean he couldn't spin a wee yarn or two. This story by him is my favourite, and tells of a little robin who desperately wanted to sing a Christmas song to the King. He knew how hazardous his long journey to meet the monarch would be, but Christmas is the time for giving, and he wanted to give the King a gift: a song, sung by himself. So off he set, with crisp, frost-covered land beneath him and bright blue sky above.

Robin and Poussie Baudrons

There was an auld gray Poussie Baudrons and she gaed awa' down by a water-side, and there she saw a wee Robin Redbreast happin' on a brier; and Poussie Baudrons says: 'Where's tu gaun, wee Robin?' And wee Robin says: 'I'm gaun awa' to the King to sing him a sang this guid Yule morning.' And Poussie Baudrons says: 'Come here, wee Robin, and I'll let you see a bonny white ring round my neck.' But wee Robin says: 'Na, na! gray Poussie Baudrons; na, na! Ye worry't the wee mousie; but ye'se no worry me.'

Robin and Grey Greedy Gled

So wee Robin flew awa' till he came to a fail fauld-dike, and there he saw a Gray Greedy Gled sitting. And Gray Greedy Gled says: 'Where's tu gaun, wee Robin?' And wee Robin says: 'I'm gaun awa' to the king to sing him a sang this guid Yule morning.' And Gray Greedy Gled says: 'Come here, wee Robin, and I'll let ye see a bonny feather in my wing.' But wee Robin says: 'Na, na! Gray Greedy Gled; na, na! ye pookit a' the wee lintie; but ye'se no pook me.'

Robin and Slee Tod Lowrie

So wee Robin flew awa' till he came to the cleuch o' a craig, and there he saw Slee Tod Lowrie sitting. And Slee Tod Lowrie says: 'Where's tu gaun, wee Robin? And wee Robin says: 'I'm gaun awa' to the King to sing him a sang this guid Yule morning.' And Slee Tod Lowrie says: 'Come here, wee Robin, and I'll let ye see a bonny spot on the tap o' my tail.' But wee Robin says: 'Na, na! Slee Tod Lowrie; na, na! Ye worry't the wee lammie; but ye'se no worry me.'

Robin and the Wee Callant

So wee Robin flew awa' till he came to a bonny burnside, and there he saw a wee callant sitting. And the wee callant says: 'Where's tu gaun, wee Robin?' And wee Robin says:

'I'm gaun awa' to the King to sing him a sang this guid Yule morning.' An the wee callant says: 'Come here, wee Robin, and I'll gi'e ye a wheen grand moolins out o' my pooch.' But wee Robin says: 'Na, na! wee callant; na, na! Ye speldert the gowdspink; but ye'se no spelder me.'

Robin Sings His Yule Sang

So wee Robin flew awa' till he came to the King, and there he sat on a winnock sole and sang the king a bonny sang. And the King says to the Queen: 'What'll we gie to wee Robin for singing us this bonny sang?' And the Queen says to the King: 'I think we'll gie him the wee Wran to be his wife.' So wee Robin and the wee Wran were married, and the King and the Queen and a' the court danced at the waddin'; syne he flew awa' hame to his ain water-side and happit on a brier.

Well, I expect all those old Scots words have you saying, 'What was that all about?' Not to worry, here it is in English.

Robin and Poussie Baudrons

There was an old grey cat called Poussie Baudrons, and she went down by the river, and there she saw little Robin Redbreast hopping on a branch; and Poussie Baudrons says, 'Where are you going little Robin?' And the Robin answers her, 'I'm on my way to sing a song for the King this fresh and bright Christmas morning.' Poussie Baudrons says, 'Come over here, little Robin, and I'll let you see a pretty white ring around my neck.' But the Robin says, 'No, no! You worry mice, but you shall not worry me.'

SOOKIN' BERRIES

Robin and the Grey, Greedy Eagle

So Robin flew away until he came to a crumbling stone wall, and there he saw a Grey, Greedy Eagle sitting on it. The Grey, Greedy Eagle says, 'Where are you going, little Robin?' And the Robin answers him, 'I'm going to sing a song for the King this fresh, bright Christmas morning.' And the Eagle says, 'Come here, little Robin, and I shall let you see a pretty feather in my wing.' But little Robin says, 'No, no! Grey Greedy Eagle; no, no! You prick all the little birds with your big beak, but you shall not prick me.'

Robin and the Sly Red Fox

So little Robin flew away until he came to some rocks, and there he saw Sly Red Fox sitting; and the Fox says, 'Where are you going, little Robin?' And little Robin answers, 'I'm going to sing a song for the King this fresh, bright Christmas morning.' And the Fox says, 'Come here, little Robin, and I shall show you a nice black furry point at the end of my tail;' But little Robin says, 'No, no! Sly Red Fox; no, no! You worry new-born lambs, but you shall not worry me.'

Robin and the Naughty Boy

So little Robin flew away until he came to a small stream, and there he saw a naughty boy sitting; and the naughty boy says to him, 'Where are you going, little Robin?' And little Robin answers, 'I'm going to sing a song for the King this fresh, bright Christmas morning.' And the naughty boy says, 'Come here, and I shall give you lots of sweeties that are in my pocket.' But the little Robin says, 'No, no! You throw stones at the spiny hedgehog, but you will not throw stones at me.'

Robin Sings His Christmas Song

So the little Robin flew away until he came to the King, and there he sat on a window sill, and sung his pretty song. And the King said to the Queen, 'What shall we give little Robin for singing so sweetly?' and she says, 'I think we should give him little Wren so that they can be married.' So little Robin and little Wren were married, and the King and Queen and all the people in the castle danced at the wedding.

6

THE CHAPMAN'S LAST PHARAOH

It is important to a teller of tales to pass on these ancient stories, not just to entertain but to share something very old. It gives me a sense of going back in time and also of handing on the tales so that they never die. Another vital factor in storytelling is group-telling. For example, one begins by laying the scene, another puts in a character, one adds another character, and one can introduce a moral which gives meat to the story. The tale soon grows and takes on a life of its own. If young people are serious and apply their imaginations, great creativity emerges. This adds the age-old conyach (heart) that brings the tale alive. In this next story I have done that. It will give you all an idea of how, from a single feather, group-telling grows wings to fly as a mighty eagle.

Many years ago in a secluded handful of crofts in the Highlands of Scotland, the quiet folk waited on a visitor. Winter brought snow and blizzards which blocked roads, making them impassable, but better was in store; ahead warm springtime sun melted ice from the mountains and all waited anxiously for news of neighbouring places.

The visitor they longed to see was the Chapman, who would know who had died, who had given birth to a baby, boy or girl, or who had moved away. He was a fine visitor to any country abode, but it was the younger generation who most keenly appreciated his presence, because this fine fellow was a storyteller. Doors were opened if by magic at his knock. Warm and welcoming food was laid upon a scrubbed table laid with best linen.

The roomiest house was chosen to entertain him in: one big enough to take all the people in the area, old and young alike. And even scruffy cats and flea-ridden dogs were captivated by the Chapman's stories, such was their depth. When night fell, surrounded by dark corners where imagined devils and goblins danced a ghostly jig to his whisperings, and when he was usually surrounded by excited faces, he told weird and wonderful tales.

I am most fortunate to have been handed down a few of his tales, and would now like to share one or two with you. Are you ready? Good – then let's go off and meet … *The Chapman*.

He was tall, with a long, flowing, dark coat, peaked hat shading a pair of slanted eyes which seemed almost closed. The heavy oak door of young Sandy's cottage shook as fist met wood; with a loud and sharp thump the visitor heralded his coming. It wasn't night time, so Sandy was allowed to answer the door. If night had fallen, it was forbidden for one so young to greet a stranger – father or older brothers did that.

'May God bless this house and all who live in it,' the Chapman said, before removing his hat. 'I have travelled many a long mile, and for the telling of a tale I would require only a small meal and a place by your welcome fire.'

Sandy's father answered, 'Be at ease, Chapman, a meal and warm seat will not be denied your good self.'

SOOKIN' BERRIES

The stranger came in as invited (he'd never set foot inside a home without invitation), removed his hat and laid it on his knee. His coat was unbuttoned as he sat down at the table. While the Chapman ate, Sandy rushed around the village, excitedly spreading the word: the storyteller was in their house, and all were welcome to come and listen.

In under an hour, everyone was hurrying to hear and be enthralled by the Chapman's tales. The old came for gossip, young women asked shyly after handsome fellows who'd taken their fancy at the hind year's market.

Without an inch of space to spare, eager children and adults sat in half-circles at his feet. Now fed and adequately warmed, the dark-skinned stranger began to speak.

'This tale, my friends, is one I heard as I passed round Bratach Castle by Loch Marla's shore.'

He moved closer to the fire, spreading a pair of stone-hard knees apart, rubbing and fanning long spindly fingers.

'It was a story like no other, and as you all know of me and my shadow-followers…' At that he lowered his heavy eyelids and looked to the floor as if waiting for a response. The boy Sandy and everyone in the room knew he meant by this the creepy demonic nightmares which plagued all listeners after a night of his special tale-telling.

His face stiffened, eyes round and protruding, and he stared at dancing flames from red hot coals burning out their hearts within the iron grate. He added, 'Not in shadows will they be found, my friends, but in careful silence. Do not make haste to steal mushrooms from their stalks – or should I be more specific – toadstools!' His face softened, as a wry smile crept slowly from ear to ear, breaking at last into a grin more of menace than of joy.

'This is not my usual kind of tale, though. Oh no, this

is a story that will make you think and wonder. It will not just be a case of my words tapping into your imagination. A thread of truth may be left behind when I'm gone from this warm and friendly home. Now can I have another cup of tea?'

The drink he requested was soon grasped in his curled fingers. He gulped half the cupful at once and then began his story.

The Last Pharaoh

On the night of the summer solstice, I sat by a tumbledown building, which many hundreds of years ago had housed dozens of soldiers of some monarch, I cannot say for sure which one. Anyway, with good heart to my campfire and a billycan to boil, I saw by the flitting moonlight a beehive-shaped gypsy wagon. It was being pulled by an overweight horse and led by a bent-backed old man. They rolled up the old winding drove road to where I sat, minding my own business, and stopped.

He was a small old man, whose days of youthful charm were long past. As he tied the leather reins to an ancient yew tree that had been twisted by sea winds, he called over, 'Hello to you, sir.'

'Same to yourself. I haven't seen you in these parts before, where do you come from?'

'I'll partake of your companionship when I gets me gry unhitched.'

I watched with wonder at the speed the grey mare was unharnessed, and in no time tethered to graze peacefully by the wagon.

'Me name is Bendigo Shadrach Jeremiah Brazil, what's your handle?'

I laughed out loud and said, 'Folks call me Chapman. Now, which of those regal-sounding handles do you want me to address you with?'

A small battered and blackened kettle was placed on my open fire before he answered. 'I call myself Bendy, and I'm from anywhere. Now does that name of yours come from the womb, or has it been given to you?'

'Your kettle's on the boil,' I said, refusing to share my birth name with a total stranger. 'Let me put a handful of tea-leaves in it for you.'

'Friend, there's nothing I'd like better.' Bendigo opened a toothless mouth, and didn't close it until it held a walnut pipe bellowing white smoke from its pot. 'I been on road most part of three days without stop, me legs are stiff and swollen, and like hamsters' cheeks are these two buttocks of mine.' He shuffled from side to side on his seat, and asked, 'You're a tale-teller?'

'Yes, I share stories with all ears about everything.'

Bendigo leaned his elbow on one knee, took a last gulp of tea and sat his cup on a flat rock. He stuffed a little more tobacco into his pipe and said, 'I have a tale for you, do you want my offering?'

How I'd longed to listen to another storyteller. There was no hesitation as I lay back on a bed of crushed bracken and beckoned my companion to tell all.

However, first there was something I had to warn him about from long experience. 'Take the floor, my fine friend. But before you begin, best I tell you of the stealthy creatures who dwell nearby. The walls of this broken keep have fissures and cracks filled with bats, and if the light from the fire is too bright, they don't half swarm about the ears.'

'That's alright, Chapman, because I'm warmed up

enough now – and as for those cloth-winged mice, they don't scare me one bit.'

I removed his hissing kettle from the flames with a stout stick, watched his gaze scan the unearthly horizon of pitch black, and wondered how far travelled this old man had been, and what sights, both of wonder and fear, he had encountered in his lifetime. His face gave away no secrets as the pipe was removed and emptied in the fire. A funnel of grey smoke sent the last puff of tobacco to journey on the loch breezes and mist.

He lowered his voice, and for a moment I thought he was trying not to disturb the bats, but there was another explanation. 'I don't want to cause stirring among the ghosts of the castle,' he said.

'No fear of that, Bendy. In all my days I never have come across any spectres or ghostly apparitions, here or anywhere.'

'There is a first time for all things,' he warned me, lowering his eyes towards the now dying embers of the fire.

As if to back up his words a fresh breeze rolled across the loch and whistled through the ruins. I felt uneasy. For a teller of tales of shadow and darkness, it throws my craft into disrepute to admit to such feelings. Nevertheless, I did shiver. He began his story.

A long time ago in ancient Egypt, a sad and weak Pharaoh, no more than twenty years of age, gathered his friends and companions around him. His lungs were sore with the effort of breathing; fluid was accumulating dangerously, blocking his airways; time for him was running out.

'My dear friends,' he said, his speech slow as every breath was another sharp pain. 'Tonight I will leave this world to take a long journey. My days are over. I called you here, not just to say goodbye, but to thank you for making my short life enjoyable. My cooks, bathers, doctors, maids, horsemen, in fact to each and every one of you, I give gratitude.'

He lay back exhausted upon his featherdown pillow. Everyone, with tear-filled eyes, cast themselves down on the floor of his bed chamber and sobbed.

'Please don't be sad,' he told them. 'This night I shall meet my parents again, and all my relatives who have gone before me. There is no need for sadness; rejoice that my pain will be gone.'

A tall muscular man stood up and said, through deep sobs, 'Sire, we are with you now, and have been every waking moment of your life. Without you, our days are not worth living. I want to come with you to the other world.'

Deeply touched by this gesture of love from his horseman, the young Pharaoh reached out and touched the sad figure gently on the cheek. Then all the others gathered around, vowing to kill themselves and find their pharaoh on the other side. It was a terrible outpouring of grief.

'Hush now, my friends. Is not the rising and setting of the desert sun a joy to behold? What of the clear waters of the great river Nile, your nourishment of goats' milk and fresh fruit, surely you cannot give these things up? Can you give up such a gift as life itself?'

One small girl, his ointment-applier, said, 'Master, we have all spoken of this day when we would lose you.' She gestured with a thin hand to the others; they gathered around her. 'Master, we wish to come with you. See –' she held out her hand to display a small vial filled with green-coloured liquid. The rest did the same.

There was no hesitation among his dearest companions.

The moment that he met death, it would not be alone. The Pharaoh was far too weak to argue, and the moment that Father Time touched his heart, all of his earthly companions swallowed their vials of poison. The whole of Egypt fell silent as each of the deceased was carried behind their master on earth, to be with their king in eternity.

Once they were on the other side of death, their pain and fear was gone. They danced and laughed in the knowledge that no more would they worry about the young Pharaoh's health; he would never know pain again, and on his journey in the other world they would be with him, as they wished.

The road they travelled seemed endless, but in that place time did not exist, so how long they'd been on their journey was anyone's guess. Every way has an ending, though, and when they saw dancing yellow lights far ahead, they rejoiced in the knowledge that they were soon to be at their destination.

On and on they went, until the light became so bright it almost closed their eyes. When the young Pharaoh saw his parents and grandparents, and his companions were reunited with their dead relatives, there was a time of merriment and wonder. Questions were asked and answered, and comparisons between the vibrant living world and the elusive other one ran off their tongues like morning dewdrops under a hot sun.

For a short time, all was peaceful, then one day a stranger came into their midst. He was a man of great height, with long, white, flowing hair and wings of an eagle. He came with news from the Almighty Spirit. 'Friends, the Great One has instructed me to put you all to sleep. A time of change is coming. His instructions must be obeyed.'

When the young Pharaoh heard this news, he called out in anger and frustration. 'I have spent all my life on earth in a state of pain and half sleep. Surely it is unjust to rob me of this new life. Here I am with all my loved ones, and now I have to sleep again.'

He felt a surge of sadness overwhelm him. His friends all rushed around to comfort and shield him.

'Can we not go and speak with the Great Spirit?' one asked the winged man.

'Yes. It is a time and yet again a time to reach his home without walls, but he is just, and will give you an audience. I have to go now, so if you are all of one mind, then please follow me.'

Without hesitation the Egyptians were once more embarked on a long journey. This time they went with uncertainty. What would the Great Spirit decide?

If there were days and nights in that world, then hundreds must have passed before they came to a place of such colour and beauty that they all thought they were in a dream. There were greens of sun-kissed forests, blues of ocean and sky, red of perfect sunsets, yellow of springtime blossoms. 'Is this heaven?' asked the young Pharaoh.

'It is the place of perfection and peace,' answered the winged man.

'Does the Great Spirit whom we seek live here?'

Suddenly every colour came together and began circling around them. Winged ladies dressed in flowing silks and satins danced to unheard of music, all keeping perfect time. It was a scene like no other; there were hundreds of them. It was the most beautiful, amazing sight.

'Who has come to my place?'

There was no person to be seen, but the voice carried into

every ear. Shaking in anticipation of being in the presence of the Great Spirit, the young Pharaoh whispered nervously, 'I have come, oh One of all things living and dead. My life on earth was a time of pain and worry. To soothe aching muscles and bones my physicians fed me sleeping potions. Oh Greatest One, why do I have to sleep here in this other world, when I did nothing but slumber in the old one?' His companions gathered round, saying nothing, but nodded in unison.

For a time no word came, until once more the winged ladies danced around in their rainbow silks, as if heralding their master's voice.

'What kind of love is this I see?' the voice asked.

'We are simply friends, one for all and all for one,' came the answer.

'I cannot send you back, surely you are aware of this. Once the cord of life is cut, it cannot be remade. But I have not met such overwhelming gratitude to a ruler from his slaves.'

'Oh no, my Lord, we are friends. I am a Pharaoh by birth, nothing more than that. Together we lived, as one we died.'

A crescendo of trumpets, harps and singing filled the air; once more the winged ladies danced and flew through a heaven of wonder. And when they had finished, they folded their wings, hung down their heads and the music quietened to a whisper.

'I shall grant your request,' said the Great Spirit, 'But to do so, I have to change a few things.'

They all gasped, and turned to the Pharaoh in anticipation of what proposals were to be made.

'I shall create another world, one between here and the

earth. Together you shall live there, and once a year, at the midnight hour of the summer solstice, I will allow you a minute to go onto the earth, to taste berries, to smell flowers and to drink water from a river's source. One last thing, I have to reduce your normal size. In this new world, I am sending you as tiny people; no taller than a mouse. Will you accept this?'

There was no question or protest. Each one lined up with eyes closed, and together they waited.

When at last their eyes opened again, the colours and silks of the winged ladies were gone.

A brand new world, with all it contained, was now theirs; to play in, laugh, sing, tell tales and live in harmony forever. As promised, from their small world, at the exact hour of the solstice, they flooded back to the earth they had left behind to smell flowers, jump upon the heath, hold hands and dance beneath rings of toadstools. Just sixty seconds, that's all the time they had. But that was enough for them, because in their world time was of no consequence.

Bendy finished his tale with a smile.

'That is the best tale I have heard in many a day,' I told him with a gentle pat on his shoulder.

Old Bendy looked behind and said, 'Was that a fluttering of cloth-wings that brushed my cheek a minute ago? Best get to bed before we are annoyed to death by those pesky bats.'

I didn't think we'd get much bother from them, because the fire had died down to a blink, and Loch Marla's breezes had been replaced by a ghostly mist which was already rolling around our ankles.

As I moved closer to the fire, my boot caught the old

billycan, spilling its dregs over the embers. Whoosh! Up and into the quiet night went a spiral of hissing steam. All around, from every broken wall of the ruined castle, came dozens of maddened bats diving head first into our bodies. We each punched the darkness, fighting with our fists the eerie menacing crowd that had encircled us. Bendy screamed, and before I knew what was happening, the poor old fellow keeled over, clutching his chest.

Hitting out at the bats, one of which had bitten a tiny chunk from my chin, I quickly bundled old Bendy up the steps of his caravan and into his beehive-shaped home. The poor old fellow's cheeks were turning from apple-red to a grey hue.

Inside the wagon and to the left was a bolted-down table, a single chair and a small stove. A neat bed was positioned at the back, and it was there I laid him down. On the right was a large kist covered with a brocade cushion, which from its dowdy appearance had seen better days. I sat on it and asked Bendy if a cup of tea would be welcome.

His lips quivered as he shook his head. It took him a few moments to find a sense of composure before he spoke. 'I'm glad I have company on this night, Chapman. There's not much breath left in this old body. Do you think it is midnight?'

I searched for a candle, and found one stuck by blobs of melted wax onto a brass lid, partly hidden behind a small pot-bellied vase containing three wooden flowers.

Bendy began to seem agitated; he stretched his neck upwards like a strangled hen reaching for its last breath.

'What time is it?' he asked.

I knew by the moon's position in the night sky that the solstice was less than ten minutes away, and told him so.

He pointed to the chest, touched my hand and whispered, 'There's a metal cup and shaving brush in that kist on which you sit. Put a little hot water in it. Me shaving soap is in the cup too. I need to look me best, Chapman. He'll soon be here.'

Now, I'm not usually so obedient to anyone, never mind an old stranger who'd just happened to come my way. But there was a gasping, gurgling sound coming from his chest. Living all my life under the star-strewn sky, I knew when death waited in the shadows. In minutes the shaving was finished, and Bendy lay silently waiting.

Something tore at my imagination, maybe the storyteller in me, I don't know, but Bendy's staring eyes, and his calmness as he waited for his lungs to give their last breath, didn't seem right. I'd seen death on many an occasion, and never was it welcome. Even dogs fight for that one last suck of air. I leaned over and whispered, 'Who is coming for you?'

'You'll see in a moment!'

An old mantel clock lay hidden under a crumpled towel which muffled its ticking. I took the towel away. As if by magic my eyes were drawn to the minute hand as it moved stealthily to touch the number twelve. Twang, the hour struck midnight – the summer solstice had come!

I heard a creaking sound and tore my eyes from the face of the clock to see, skipping and dancing in the wagon door, a line of the tiniest people I had ever seen, each one no bigger than my thumb. I rubbed my eyes. Was this real? Was Bendigo a magician? Was I about to wake up and find myself sitting at the fire, sipping tea and listening to snoring bats?

Transfixed I watched as the throng of little people formed into two lines. Running as fast as he could, a man wearing gold cuffs and a large necklace filled with every precious gem there is, leapt from my foot onto my knee, and from this vantage point skipped across my shoulder to land gently on Bendy's chest. It was easy to see that this was the regal Pharaoh my companion had told me about. I was definitely in the company of a wonderful illusionist, who was not only faking death, but had conjured up a vision of tiny people. It was easy to see that his story contained hidden hypnotic words, and I was being hypnotised.

'Come now, Bendigo, we've only a few seconds!' The supposed once great king of Egypt summoned my friend to rise from his bed, and of course he did. I sat back without a word, and watched this mystical magician, who thought he was still in control of my mind, shrink from normal to miniature size. He waved goodbye, and went off with his tricksters out of the caravan door and into the night.

I followed him out there into the darkness, but there was no sign of anyone. I laughed loudly, and called to him, 'The best storyteller in the world, that's what you are Bendy, me old pal. You can come back now. I was well and truly fooled there for a moment. Whoever heard of a Chapman wool-eyed?'

I waited, but apart from the ever-growing mist and one lone bat fluttering above my head there was nothing to be seen, my old friend stayed hidden. 'He'll let me simmer a while before his shaky legs come wandering back,' I told myself, yawning at the same time. Hour followed hour until sleep rendered me unconscious. I woke early to the swooping, not of bats, but of sand martins eagerly feeding on the clouds of midges who in turn were happily feeding off me.

'Bendy,' I called, stepping into the wagon, 'why did you

let me sleep on the cold ground without a cover?' Everything was exactly the same as I'd left it. Where had he gone?

Down at the loch side, as I refilled my billycan, I scanned every corner from tree-lined shore to high hills, and searched inside and outside the castle ruins. I even saddled up the old grey mare and searched for miles. All day and on into the night I searched, but Bendy had completely disappeared.

More and more puzzled by events, I built a fire and cooked some small trout which I'd guddled in the shallow water. Then, after I had eaten, a thought came to mind that I hadn't checked underneath the wagon. Dropping onto my knees, I crawled between the wheels, and what I found there convinced me for the rest of my life of one thing – Bendigo was no illusionist! In soft sand, a perfect line of tiny footprints went from below the steps, under the wagon and ended at its edge!

What had been to me a fine piece of trickery was in essence the point blank truth. There are indeed little people, and how Bendy knew of them is a secret he never divulged. But as you ponder my story, think on this – who else knows of them, where have they come from, and is the word as we know it, FAIRY, really PHARAOH?

'Well, my friends, thank you for the hospitality, most welcome as always.'

Young Sandy stood up, wide-eyed and breathless at having heard such a wondrous tale, and said, 'Chapman, what did you do with the old man's caravan?'

'Now, that's the strangest thing, because next day, before I packed my things to take to the road, I woke to a pile of smouldering ashes where the caravan had been. The beehive wagon had mysteriously burned as I slept. On my travels

I have heard that gypsies burn all that is left by their dead. I did bring one thing to show you though.' Everyone followed the Chapman outside to see, happily grazing on the hillside, an old grey mare with plenty of good ploughing left in her shanks.

The Chapman's Lost Blessing

7

FOXES SHOULD BE FREE

We will visit the Chapman again later, but for now I want to share a lovely story with you about how, when we do a good turn, it sometimes is appreciated and returned in kind.

Several years ago my feet were weary. I'd advertised on the oral grapevine for travelling people's stories. I sought life stories, personal events memorised for sharing, moral tales with an aaahh factor. From the rugged coastline, where sea winds batter the walls of John o' Groats, to Galloway and Dumfries in the Borders, came phone calls, emails and letters. I trekked from retired church beadles to tale-keepers among old farmworkers, recording and noting as many stories as I could.

My fingers grew stiff trying to keep up with some of my more sprightly tellers, who swore certain paragraphs were true, only to insist I change them because they weren't sure. When walking with a certain shepherd who insisted he could only tell stories when gathering in his flocks, my legs got so lame I thought I'd walk forever bandy. It was the best feeling in the whole world, however, when I got home to the computer, and stories began falling methodically into place. All the aches and pains were worth it to me, just to know that those wonderful tales would live forever in the pages of my books.

Here's a tale that ticks all boxes regarding human / animal bonding. That age old moral saying comes to mind – 'one good turn deserves another'.

Izzy and her grandparents had been on the road for the best part of four months. With winter rapidly approaching, their burdens would soon be unloaded in a snug campsite in one of the honourable Mr Murray's forests.

For all of Wullie's life, he'd worked during the winter for the kindly landowner, and although older now and slightly bent-backed, he'd a strong resolve. His duties would be to help on the grouse moors of Ochtertyre estate helping the gamekeeper control vermin, and many other tasks. This stately home was run for hundreds of years by the Murrays, who were closely related to the Dukes of Atholl, who in turn are related to the Queen. His wage would be five shillings a week, plus his fill of fowl and fish from the nearby River Earn.

Izzy wasn't the couple's kin. They had found her wrapped in an old shawl laid by the busy roadside on the old A9. Today it's a wider, faster road, and the babe in her swaddling clothes would almost certainly have been run over by a heavy goods vehicle. However, in the late nineteenth century, the traffic was only horse and carriage. Where she came from they never discovered. They simply lifted her up, held her close, and for twelve years never let her go.

They were two honest and sober parents for her, and she was a lovely daughter for them. Her charm, which delighted them daily, was in her devotion to every living creature, even the rabbits that Wullie snared for their supper. She would skin and prepare the beasts, thanking them for the sustenance provided. Izzy only left their sight when meandering through the countryside where no harm could befall her.

It was mid-November when they set up camp. Wullie wasted no time in reporting to the big house to be given his winter duties, which, along with his grouse-moor work, included shoeing horses, bagging fox-furs and deerskins for the market, snaring vermin – his workload was endless.

As he headed down the rhododendron-lined driveway of the stately mansion, he heard a horse come galloping up behind him, and if he'd not leapt out of the way, he would most certainly been mowed down. The rider didn't even apologise, but laughed and mocked him for being in his way.

'Stupid stuffed pork pig of a man,' he thought, eyeing a pair of well rounded buttocks. 'Just as fat as the horse's rear end, that one,' he mused.

The horseman gripped the reins and pulled the bit in the horse's mouth tight into its chest, so that it snorted loudly. Wullie, who thanked God daily for Jenny his old cart horse, shouted out, 'That's no way to treat a beast of burden!'

In a flash the rider dismounted, strode over to where Wullie stood, lifted a knotted leather whip above his head and struck the poor unsuspecting man over the shoulders. 'I'll have you thrashed to within an inch of your miserable life for such insolence!' Clicking the heels of two calf-leather boots, he stared down at the whipped man, who was shaking violently. 'What are you doing on private land anyway?'

Wullie straightened his spine and tried hard not to show the fear welling up in his body. 'Sir, I come here every year to work for Mr Murray. He allows me to winter my tent in the woods. We have been coming for many years, the wife and me.'

Like a prowling dog the horseman walked round, eyeing him up. He leaned closer until both men's noses almost touched. Wullie felt the hot breath on his face, then a spray of wet air. 'Tent, a tinker? Well, filthy little vagabond, hear this and pay heed to my words. My uncle, your so-called Mr Murray, is in South Africa, and will be there for a considerable time. I am in sole charge of the land and everything you see. So go back to your filthy abode and shift from here, or, so help me, I'll have you burned off!'

What a shock this was to a man with an elderly wife and child to provide for. He knew any amount of pleading to this heartless creature would fall on deaf ears. He'd seen that same face on a thousand landowners and factors, and heard the same venom. It would be devastating news for Annie and Izzy, but when a man keeps a stone for a heart, reasoning is futile.

He turned and walked back down the road, his good spirits dispersed to the wind as the thumping of the horse's hooves on the gravel path faded with its rider. As he walked the weary way back through the woods, Izzy, who was gathering a variety of wild mushrooms, met him. Words between them weren't necessary; he'd a hang-dog look, a 'can't stay here' stare.

'Grandaddy,' she said softly, 'is Mr Murray dead?'

'No, lassie, he's out of the country'

'Who said we have to leave?' She knew the procedure, had witnessed it many times. Many times she'd seen his hunched shoulders, bonnet scrunched in his fist. She knew he'd been rejected. 'Is there a new factor? I'll go and speak with him and tell him just what a fine worker you are.'

'I don't know what manner of creature he is, but I'd guess his mother forgot to take the silver spoon from his mouth.

He's a bad un, lassie. And you will not approach such a man. Come help me break the news to Grandmammy.'

There was a cosy fire at the tent mouth, Jenny the mare was tethered to a gnarled oak tree, the kettle was hissing its welcome from the spout to say that tea would soon be ready. It was such a homely sight neither wanted to tell Annie the bad news. But she too saw the obvious 'no welcome' sign on their faces.

'He's passed on then, Mr Murray. Who's the new owner?' she asked in a matter-of-fact manner, resigned to her fate of weary winter-travelling ahead. 'How long do we have before we have to move on?'

'No time at all, wife. And no, the master isn't finished, but I sure wish his stand-in factor was. He's a right brute, and I've met enough in my time to be ready to go when ordered.'

'God help us then, Wullie, because when I was filling the kettle at the burnside a lip of ice was forming among the reeds. Snow will be here, and well before we get any distance away. It's fine if the onslaught of winter is mild, but in these parts, as you well know, she burls a hardy broom.'

Izzy loved her adopted parents more than anything in the world, and the thought of them suffering under a blanket of snow, or worse still, caught in a snowdrift, was too much for her to bear. Turning on her heels she bounded off towards the big house, with cries that she should not approach the stranger ringing in her ears. Maybe if she spoke to the man, reasoned with him, then he'd change his mind and let them stay.

As she picked up her feet and bounded on, tears of concern for Wullie and Annie filled her eyes and dimmed her vision. Unable to avoid a fence-post, down she went, gravel tearing into her knee. 'Ouch,' she screamed, examining the bloodied wound, 'the last thing I needed was this.'

To stem the blood loss she tore a strip of cotton from the hem of her already tattered dress and bound the knee. For a while it was too painful to stand on, and sitting quietly nursing her injury she was aware of rustling in the nearby undergrowth. Curious to see who or what it was, she ignored the trickle of blood and got up to investigate.

It didn't take long for her to see a young vixen snared tightly, held secure between two silver birch trees. The captive animal wasn't moving. She knew that when foxes run into snare wire they usually try to struggle free, but being the cleverest of forest creatures, when they realise the futility of such an attempt, they become resigned to their fate, and sit quietly waiting for death. If the maker of the snare is conscientious he will check them every day, but if not then death comes very cruelly and painfully slowly. This little vixen seemed to have given up the struggle, but when she saw Izzy approach, she pulled frantically, tightening the noose. Her eyes bulged and she began gasping for air.

Forgetting her painful wound, Izzy dropped to her knees, moving closer to the animal. 'There now, poor wee thing, I mean you no harm. Stay very still and I'll soon have that horrible wire loose.'

The fox knew by Izzy's soothing tone she'd not come as an enemy, and stopped straining at the wire. On a bed of red oak leaves she rested her exhausted body and allowed Izzy to prise open the snare. The plucky vixen felt the wire release its death grip and wasted no time. She wriggled free, and in a flash of red fur had gone, leaving her rescuer with an overwhelming sense of well being and of being at one with nature.

This didn't last, however, as behind her an angry voice boomed, 'What the hell are you up to?'

Terrified, she scrambled from the undergrowth, stood up on two wobbling legs and leant back unsteadily against a tree trunk. 'I was looking for mushrooms, sir.'

'Are you aware that you are trespassing?' He cast a disapproving glance at her torn dress and bleeding knee. A brisk wind was removing the last autumn leaves which pattered down around her, adding a will o' the wisp appearance to the frightened child.

'Are you the gamekeeper's girl?' he asked, lifting her elfin chin with the handle of his leather whip.

'I'm a tinker lass who wants to speak to Mr Murray's man.'

'Oh you are, are you? Well, filthy vermin child, talk away!'

All courage or any sense of affinity with the earth drained from her thin body and disppeared into the soil beneath her feet. She was already walking back the way she had come. There was no mystery – this was the beast who'd whipped her granddaddy, and who without a doubt would do the same to her.

'Wait a minute, I'm not finished with you.' With the whip, which seemed like an extension to his arm, he parted the low-lying bushes. 'I wouldn't believe a single word that came from a tinker's mouth. What were you up to, slinking in there?'

His breeches were far too tight, and as he leaned down to look, Izzy almost forgot her fear and laughed loudly at the size of his buttocks. When he discovered the opened snare, all hell was let loose. 'I'll skin you alive for this!' he cried.

His shouts and threats were fading in the distance, as Izzy ran faster than she'd ever done before into the arms of Annie. All the packing was finished. Jenny, the mare, was hitched onto the small cart.

'Lassie, I hope you didn't meet the boss man,' Wullie said, leading Jenny onto the track.

'Well, Grandaddy, I think I did!'

Annie lost her head on seeing the line of deep red blood congealed on Izzy's leg and thought the worst. 'He's attacked our wee lassie! I'll find the pig and sink a wild curse onto his skull for hurting my precious!' A burnt stick discarded from the campfire was retrieved, each cardigan sleeve rolled over the elbow, and off she went to seek the beast of Ochtertyre.

'Woman,' called Wullie, running after her, 'don't do anything silly.'

Izzy chased after them both, explaining that her cut knee had nothing to do with the boss man, but before the three of them had made any ground towards the big house, the man himself appeared. He was sporting a fine rifle, with two more marksmen on either side, and he met them head on.

'Now, sir, we seem to have got ourselves tangled up in a web of misunderstandings. Can you not see your way to changing your mind and letting us stay? I can do any amount of tasks.' Wullie felt there should be some way of reasoning with the man.

He quickly removed his bonnet, held it tightly in his fist, and began to reel off the crafts and skills he had for working on a shooting estate. Izzy and Annie watched the twitching, sneering face of the brute who was masquerading as a fine gentleman.

'Come away from this place, man. Sure, that buttock-faced chap has no intentions of letting us stay. He's toying with us.' Annie was a proud woman and was not about to bow her head for anyone, especially this broad-shouldered fellow with his fiery red eyes, puffed cheekbones and lip adorned with a thin moustache.

'Right, lads,' was all the reply Wullie got. 'Set fire to the tent, I'll shoot the horse!'

Annie screamed. 'The tent's all packed up, so no need to fire anything!' She tried to stop the man striding towards their only means of transport, but he was already getting his rifle ready to shoot. 'Oh my goodness, surely not!'

She, Izzy and Wullie knew they would get nowhere without Jenny, and ran forward, pleading and begging with the factor not to kill the horse. He was already round the bend in the track road where the unsuspecting Jenny munched at the verge, eyes half-closed and oblivious to the events unfolding. The factor lifted the rifle to aim, his henchmen pulling back the family of terrified onlookers.

Then, just as his finger pulled the trigger, the strangest thing happened. Out of the undergrowth came a flash of red fur, right into the sights of the murder weapon. The gun shot wildly up into the heavens as the boss man fell back into the path, banging his head on a big round boulder. Immediately his henchmen rushed to his aid, while Willie, Annie and Izzy tore off down the track with Jenny almost in full gallop.

'Grandaddy, did you see the fox?'

'Aye, lassie, that I did. I've never in all my born days seen such a thing. Do you think it was in the undergrowth and thought the gun was meant for him?'

'No, I think it was helping us!' Izzy didn't tell her grand-dad she'd opened a snare and deliberately let the animal go free. He'd not be too pleased, and would have blamed that for their sudden departure from their wintering ground. Anyway, more pressing matters lay ahead – where they were to stay now, and how to survive.

They'd gone about four miles along the ever-bending track, when behind them the sound of horses' hooves could be heard, growing louder as it got nearer. 'Jenny, over lass,' said Wullie, and he guided his mare off the track just in time to avoid a light carriage careering towards them.

It was pulled by a high-necked stallion, black as night, showing the whites of its eyes and snorting like a spooked dragon. 'Watch out there!' screamed a woman who was holding desperately onto the reins for dear life. 'I can't stop, he's terrified, mind out!'

Unable to stop the horse themselves, they watched help-lessly as it galloped down the hill.

Halfway down, the road bent slightly, and for the second time that day they witnessed an unexplained phenomenon. Almost as if in flight, the same fox appeared out of the bushes and tore into the path of the runaway horse. It reared up on its hind legs, neighing madly and giving the woman just enough time to control it and halt its deadly ride. Two minutes more, and both horse and buggy would have col-lided with a fallen tree further down the way.

That was when Izzy confessed about her escapade of freeing the fox. 'It came to help us, Granddaddy, honest! You've said it yourself, Grandmother – "one good turn deserves another!"'

Once the woman had calmed herself, she alighted from her buggy and spoke to the tinkers. 'Did any of you kind people see the red fox?'

'We all saw it, ma'am,' answered Wullie, 'but in all my

life living close to Mother Earth, I can say in all honesty that never have I seen such a thing. Today we saw this twice. Earlier it saved our Jenny over there.' Willie pointed to the old mare, already being approached by the handsome stallion which was trying to nibble from her nose bag. 'Under threat of death from a senseless gent too fond of his own voice, a fox put itself in the line of fire and, well, you might think me daft, but it looked as if the sly thing was saving our horse from the gun.'

'And your life too, Missus!' shouted breathless Izzy.

'The countryside and its inhabitants are a law unto themselves. I have always had the greatest respect for my fellow-creatures.'

The woman, who was middle-aged, wearing a green velvet coat with bonnet to match, then asked them why they were still on the road. She added, 'My knowledge of you people is that, living in a tent, all your winter roots must be down before first snowfall. I saw ice in the pond today – surely you're late wintering.'

Wullie looked at Annie and Izzy, but it was the youngster who spoke first. 'My granddad always winter works for Mr Murray. We've been told by a right brute of a man that our kind isn't welcome there now. It seems the master is away.'

'Yes, as an officer with the army in Africa. It is a terrible business, the Boer War, my husband is away too. That nasty piece of work you speak of is the honourable Mr Percy Wotheringham, nephew to the laird. When he returns next summer he'll be ever so angry with him. Many neighbours have complained about his behaviour. Where are you going to go?' She seemed quite concerned, and added that tinkers were worth their weight in gold, given all their knowledge of horses and the land.

Wullie knew, however, they had several more miles to travel before camping down for the night. He'd no idea where they'd find a welcome, one that offered work, so he replied vaguely, thanking the lady for her kind words. Izzy and Annie did the same.

Watching them trudge off down the track, heads bent, the lady suddenly had an idea, and called after them to wait. 'You can live in the forest on my land.'

Wullie, thinking the woman was a good-hearted soul who didn't wish to see them wander aimlessly, replied, 'It's kind of you, mistress, but I'm a proud man. My wife and Izzy are not beggars. We think you're a nice lady, but don't give us shelter if there is no work for us.'

'With half my workforce fighting in the war, there's plenty of chores needing done. The fences are in a dreadful state, my shepherd will need extra hands at the lambing and there's wool needs to be bagged, rabbits controlled and this big horse is too large for me to control. Do you wish me to continue?' She smiled and held out her gloved hand. 'Lady Culzean at your service,' she said politely.

Annie smiled at Wullie, whose head was nodding vigorously. 'We shall be very pleased to take up your offer, mistress.' Immense relief spread across his wrinkled brow as they walked back with the lady, who they later discovered was a rich landowner. She owned the neighbouring estate to that of Mr Murray.

Happily they followed her into a nice enclosure in a patch of woodland, from where the spires of her stately home could clearly be seen. She helped them unroll their canvas abode, and even helped erect the tent.

The old tent, however, had seen better days, and when she saw the gaping holes in its sides she offered them a vacant cottage next door to the shepherd, a Mr Dougie Gardiner.

Life for the family from that day took on a whole new meaning. Lady Culzean became not just an employer but a dear friend. Sadly, Annie took a stroke that winter and was unable to continue her wandering ways. They never went back on the road again.

Izzy grew strong and learned the ways of livestock and moorland management, loving every minute of it. Some days she'd fill a flask of tea, pack a few sandwiches and take off. She knew every nook and cranny of the estate. Lady Culzean, who had no family, sent her to university, and from there she entered into a life of veterinary practice.

She spent her life travelling the world studying the many varieties of wildlife, from lions in the Serengeti desert to poisonous snakes in the Amazonian swamps.

After Wullie and Annie passed away, she seldom found the time to go home to Culzean, but when she did, locals spoke fondly of the tall woman who spoke to foxes.

8

BULLIES

Bullies were everywhere when I was a child. Sometimes they waited for me outside school, sometimes inside. I was terrified. However as I grew older I began to look upon them not so much as something to be frightened of but as a pesky problem. If approached properly such problems can be defeated, it's just a matter of how much you want rid of them.

By the time I'd reached the age of twelve, people told me I had become quite a good storyteller. This next story about bullying would have appealed to me at that time. Although it is for younger readers, it has a message for us all.

In the forest of the Fairy Queen, trees, plants and animals lived in perfect harmony. She wouldn't tolerate anything that upset the peace of her pretty woodlands. Every so often she'd send out her fairy helpers to check that all was as it should be.

At the entrance to the forest, two giant oaks stood tall and strong; their thick branches spreading upwards to catch the sun's rays and the rain's welcoming waters. Birds came in springtime to build their nests there, and in summer they raised healthy chicks. During the day, their branches were a favourite resting place for wise old owl, the watcher of the woods, and in the night his eyes could see everything that moved about down below on the forest floor.

Harmony reigned supreme, until one very upsetting day. Helgalum the witch, famous for causing trouble, was gathering some herbs and mushrooms, when she stopped under the shade of the oaks to rest. 'These two trees have grown to a giant size, they'd make perfect fuel for my stove,' she thought, admiring the thickness of their brown trunks and relishing the thought of how much warmth she'd get as they burned in her fireplace. She pictured them cut into logs and piled neatly outside her cottage wall.

'Not much chance of that, though,' she thought. She remembered the last time she had helped herself to a few branches of fresh green broom for a new broomstick that she wanted to use to fly to the moon on. The Fairy Queen's helper had seen her cutting down chunks of the broom, and she shivered at the thought of the powerful wind the Queen had sent to blow her into space. Helgalum would still be circling Mars if she'd not managed to attach herself to a comet heading for Earth. She hoped the Queen's helpers weren't around as she rested, but oh dear, the sudden swish of an oak branch reminded her of how keen-eyed the little fairies were.

'Does Her Majesty know that you're back?' enquired one of them, staying out of reach of Helgalum's long arm. She would swat them like flies if they got too near her.

'I arrived back last week from my wonderful trip among the planets, and if she didn't hear about it then, she will now.'

'You had better get out of her forest and back to your

swamp, if you know what's good for you,' the little fairies all shouted. They shouted so loud, both oaks awakened and shook their heavy branches, which in turn woke up the wise old owl.

'What is going on in our peaceful forest?' he asked angrily.

'Helgalum has arrived back on earth, and is trespassing again!' said both trees in unison.

Realising that at any minute news of her arrival would reach the Queen, Helgalum pulled a black cloak over her humpy shoulders, lifted her basket of herbs and mushrooms, and slunk off into the undergrowth, muttering, 'Can a poor old witch not get a rest in this place?'

'You go and rest in your swamp,' shouted both oaks, watching her disappear.

When the Queen heard that Helgalum had come back, she posted extra guards at every entrance to her forest kingdom, and told everyone to be watchful of the foolish old witch and her naughty ways.

Helgalum may have been old, but foolish she certainly wasn't. She wanted those trees, and was willing to wait until she could work out how to get them. Trees could not be touched by her magic, and she didn't have normal human energy to cut them down, so she had to find a way to cause problems.

After a while tossing on her crow-feathered mattress, as outside her cottage creatures of the swamp howled, a brilliant thought came to mind. She would break the harmony between the trees. If the trees didn't get on, then the Queen would have them sent to the swamp's forest, where all naughty trees were sent. Once they were in there, Helgalum would have power over them and she would pay the swamp men to cut them down. And as she sat in bed resting her pointy chin on knobbly knees, she knew just what to do.

Troggle, the tree on the right, gently tapped his twin, Friggle, to wake him up. The sun was shining, the birds singing happily. Both gave their large branches a gentle shake, then wished the birds, squirrels and old owl a bright good morning, before stretching up towards the warming sun.

Down below, an elderly lady who was gatherering sticks smiled and said, 'What a lovely day it is, and my goodness, what a handsome pair you are.' She was, of course, referring to the oaks, who smiled and nodded in agreement.

As she stooped down to pick up some broken twigs, the old lady whispered to Troggle, 'But you are the best-looking.' She then walked around the other side and paid exactly the same compliment to Friggle, and then wandered off.

Now, everyone in the forest knew not to pay compliments to anyone else – Her Majesty forbade it. It was her rule that no one was better or worse than any other in her kingdom, all were equal. So when the trees began to argue about who was the best-looking, word soon reached her ears. There were stories about how Troggle would shake his branches violently at Friggle, trying to break his branches. This resulted in poor mother birds losing their precious freshly built nests. Then she heard that old owl had almost fallen to the ground head–first, because Friggle had stretched too high attempting to stop Troggle getting sunshine. The trees shouted and roared so much that not a single squirrel, bird, rabbit, deer, badger, hoppy frog, fox or any other kind of creature would go near them. Soon the Queen and her fairies decided the bickering was causing disharmony, and it had to stop.

As she arrived at the entry to the forest, a dreadful sight met the Queen's eyes. Broken branches lay scattered among piles of fallen green leaves, scratches zig-zagged each of their trunks.

'Look at the state of you,' she screamed at them – she was very angry. All through the usually peaceful forest, the whispering and murmuring from tree-tops to rabbit burrows spread like wildfire. 'What is going on here?' she asked, pointing her silver wand at each of the oaks.

'I am very handsome,' said Troggle, proudly, 'but Friggle won't accept the fact.'

'That's a lie! Everyone knows I am much better-looking than you. On the right I grow, sun to rise and rain to flow.'

'That's rubbish! I face left towards the east, and on the sunshine do I feast.'

Troggle grinned cheekily at his twin, who said, 'Whatever!'

The Queen was not amused, but she could see this was not the normal way for her creatures to behave. Someone must have started this, and it didn't take much thought to know who. 'My children, what has caused such puffed up pride between you both? Has there been a stranger sneaking around?'

Both trees agreed that only an old stick-gatherer had come by. Then, as each thought about her visit, it occurred to them that she had whispered to each that he was handsome. Friggle and Troggle stared at each other, and in unison they said, 'Helgalum!'

'Yes, just as I thought, that nasty witch has plans for you both. She probably wants to burn you in her fire.'

Everywhere in the forest the sound of an oohh! could

be heard. The Fairy Queen knew that her oaks could not be left at the mercy of Helgalum's schemes, so she decided to plant a new tree between them. This would stop them thinking only of themselves.

She waved her wand in the air, and suddenly a tiny fir tree lifted its little head from the soil between Friggle and Troggle. A gentle breeze blew, lulling the new babe to sleep.

'There now, that is done. I command you both to protect and nourish this little tree, that I name Gregba. If I so much as hear a whisper that you are not taking good care of him, then I shall personally see to it that you are chopped down and given as a present to Helgalum herself. Do I make myself clear?'

The Fairy Queen lifted her wand and twirled it in the air. She didn't do that unless she meant business. There was a shaking of branches and nodding of trunks in answer to her very serious command.

For a week or two, peace reigned, much to Helgalum's annoyance.

Then something happened. Friggle and Troggle had a serious conversation. Gregba was growing. His prickly pine needles were making their trunks itch. If he grew as tall as they were, he'd steal their sunshine and rain water. He had to be kept small.

The Queen wouldn't hear of her new baby tree being uprooted, so it was up to them. They began to bully the sapling. The first thing they did was to join their branches above his head, to stop rain feeding his top boughs and to keep out the sun.

Soon the sad little tree began to feel weak, but when he complained, the oaks would smack him with their powerful branches. They'd squeeze him with their trunks so he could hardly breathe. Before long, the life of Gregba hung in the balance.

Helgalum, meanwhile, decided she could wait no longer. She summoned two swamp men and ordered them to take sharp saws and cut down the two oaks standing at the forest entrance.

It was a very dark night, perfect for such a task. Thump, thump, went the heavy green feet of the monsters of the murky deep as they made tracks from the swamps to the forest. 'Stop that thumping!' Helgalum hissed. 'Tip-toe,' she ordered, 'or I'll turn you into puff-faced toads.'

So, moving as quietly as possible, the evil threesome made their way towards the unsuspecting oaks.

Gregba, though, wasn't feeling well. He'd been bullied severely by both trees, and was nursing a sore branch when he saw the creatures approaching, led by the wicked witch. 'Oh dear,' he said, and began to shake with fear.

He watched the swamp men measuring up the trunks of sleeping Friggle and snoring Troggle. Helgalum walked up and down whispering orders. It was then that the light from the full moon, high in the night sky, lit up the shiny saw. Teeth as sharp as eagle's talons were placed silently against Friggle.

'Oh dear, they're going to cut down the trees, I must try and stop them!' With his last remaining strength, little Gregba began flapping his branches against both oak's trunks, screaming, 'Wake up, the witch is here! Look out, you two, they are cutting you down!'

Friggle yawned and opened his eyes. Troggle did the same. Then, when they saw both swamp creatures and Hegalum, they bashed and lashed and walloped them so hard that the swamp men were sent flying through the air to land in a monster puddle, sending gallons of sticky yukky mud squirting upwards.

Helgalum screamed as she saw thousands of fairies converge on the spot where all the commotion was coming from. Seconds later, Her Majesty appeared. 'You!' she gasped, seeing the witch with big woodcutting saws at her feet. 'Is there no teaching you?' She lifted her wand stiffly above her head and said, 'Moon, send a beam for Hegalum. Take her to your dark side, so that she will never find her way back to our forest.'

Hegalum hated space, with its black holes and burning stars. 'Oh lovely queen, if I give you my promise never to come into your kingdom again, will you allow me to go home to the swamp?' She was on her knees, hands clasped tightly, begging to remain.

'Well, perhaps there is a way you can stay on earth,' said the Queen, swirling her wand above Hegalum's head. 'Green as moss and round as moon, turn the witch into a spoon!'

In a flash Hegalum turned into a spoon. She was taken by the fairies and given as a gift to the underwater King of the Swamps. He too had become fed up with her tricks, and was delighted now to be able to sup his soup with a brand new shiny spoon.

From that day, all was peaceful in the forest. And as for the two bullying oaks, well, they were so grateful to tiny Gregba for saving their lives, they spent every moment catching the rain and sunshine and feeding his trunks and branches. They were like doting parents, much to the pleasure of Her Majesty, Queen of the Forest.

9

THE CURSE OF SCOTLAND

Here is another story about the aftermath of the Battle of Culloden, when the Jacobites under Bonny Prince Charlie were defeated in their attempt to overthrow King George II. According to many tellers of this tale, the events described in it really happened.

After the battle, the victorious Duke of Cumberland decided to go to the house where Bonny Prince Charlie had stayed on the day before the battle, and to sleep in the Prince's bed. This would show who now held power in the land. A large mansion on the outskirts of Inverness was where this took place, and here the story unfolds.

To tell the whole story it is necessary to go back to the night before the battle, to a room where the Prince and his generals were playing cards.

A sharp breeze had picked up wandering sea spray and was blowing it inland and onto the moorland around the house. Somewhere not too far off, an owl hooted. Folks called his hooting the song of silence, because it was a signal that the big eyes of the night predator had detected food. This was likely to be a mouse, a vole or a poor wee garden warbler.

Every little creature stopped and stiffened, hoping and praying the talons of the old owl would not sink into their vulnerable necks, hence the silence that followed his call.

Prince Charlie peered from a window on the first floor into the darkness and listened. 'It's quiet out there,' he said softly. The horizon bristled with young tree-tops like tiny pyramids, prompting him to add, 'If only they were soldiers.' He'd been informed by his advisers that many Highlanders would come to swell the numbers of his army. A great force of strong men would arrive on Culloden Moor, that was a certainty, and would chase the Duke of Cumberland back across the border. Charlie thought that he'd be flying his banner as he marched into Edinburgh next week, as soon as they'd won the war in Scotland.

One of his trusted generals called to him, 'Come away, Sire, from the window. There are unseen enemies who'd put a hole in you with a fair-aimed gun filled with lead. See, we have a pack of cards, let's play awhile.'

No matter how much his trusty advisors encouraged him, his heart felt heavy-laden. Ever since an earlier attempt on his life back in Crieff, when he'd been rushed out of the Drummond Arms and into Ferntower House, he'd felt a sense of foreboding, and it could not be shaken off. He was no fool; he'd seen the mountainous terrain where the battle would be fought and seen how many Highlanders and others who were faithful followers of his cause would make up his army. He knew that a fight against the mighty Duke's well-fed, well-equipped troops would be no pushover. Oh, his men had plenty of heart, but stamina in war comes from decent meals. His men hadn't eaten for days, or slept either. But next day's battle would decide once and for all what path Scotland would travel.

'Sire, I say again, will you partake of a quiet game of cards?'

The Prince smiled and said, pointing to the solitary candle lit in the centre of the table, 'Indeed, but what of this light? It's barely a flicker. I can hardly see your faces, let alone a card.'

'It will help to while away the hours, Sire,' answered his General, sitting astride a wobbly-legged chair. 'Who will be able to find sleep this night?'

'Who indeed, my friend? Now deal my hand, and if tomorrow I lose, tonight I shall win.'

The Prince seemed cheerful, but he was deliberately hiding the inner turmoil of his heavy heart.

A gentle spotting of rain tip-tapped on the window. The Prince had had a grand run of pontoon – seven, eight, nine, ten, jack and queen, all cards in the same suit. Everyone laid their cards down; the Prince, raising an eyebrow, smiled and said, 'I will see you all.' He leaned over to spread his cards on the table, but one slipped from his grasp and fell into the darkness below the table. 'Oh my! Don't anyone say a word,' he ordered, 'until I have retrieved my card.' He looked for the card under the table, but it was nowhere to be seen. Lifting the table they all searched for it by the flickering candlelight, but it had gone.

'Well, that is a pity, because without it I cannot win this hand.' He dismissed the card players, saying it was very late. All should have a night's sleep and be refreshed for the battle.

One of his generals, Hector MacKay, a faithful Irish follower of the Stuart cause, was a very superstitious man. Although he said nothing at the time, the night's card game left him deeply fearful about the oncoming battle. The card that had been lost was the nine of diamonds, and nine was an ominous number in his part of Ireland – a signal of doom.

As we know from history, the fight was indeed lost. Prince Charles Edward Stuart escaped and fled to France. Culloden Moor, where the fallen Highlanders and others who had rallied to the Stuart flag found their graves, was to be the final battlefield on British soil. The date was 16 April 1745.

But as I said at the beginning of this story, to the victor goes the spoils. In Cumberland's case, his desire was to lodge in the same houses as his foe. The night after Charlie had escaped, the Duke slept peacefully in the bed the Prince had occupied before the battle. The next morning he assembled all his troops to give them their orders. He summoned his generals. 'From this day forward, I will not tolerate any wearing of the tartan. Everyone must learn to speak the King's English. And most important, I command that you take enough men, go forth and kill every Highlander you meet – the old, women and children – spare no one. Set fire to the land; torch every house you see. Once and for all, the clans must be dispersed.'

A general named David Bowles Prentice stepped forward and said, 'It is a bold thing you ask of us, Sir, but I will not carry out such a dire order unless you write it down and sign it.'

Cumberland was in no mood to be disobeyed. 'Mr Prentice, you will do as I say!'

Prentice was, however, a soldier of the King, and there were rules which had to be observed. He repeated his request, adding that in the service of the King, protocol must be adhered to.

'Oh, very well, get me a pen and paper,' ordered Cumberland. But there was nothing left in the house, not even a cup or saucer. Even the bed had been stripped and was gone. The house had been ransacked; the looters had left it bare.

He shouted at his waiting generals to forget about written orders and to get on with it. He was tired of Scotland and wanted to go home. But they, like Prentice, said that they would do the job, but only once they had it in writing. In a fit of temper the Duke hurled away his chair and thumped his boot hard on the floor. This disturbed a square of carpet, revealing something underneath. He bent down and retrieved the lost nine of diamonds. 'This will do,' he shouted. And there on the card he scribbled the order, 'Kill them! Signed by his hand, Duke of Cumberland, second son of his Royal Majesty.'

From that day to this, the nine of diamonds has been referred to as 'The Curse of Scotland'.

10

THE PROUD HIGHLANDER

Scotland has a wonderful collection of old tales about the last battle ever fought on her soil, and here is one more. This tale is from a time when travellers went under the name of tinkers – workers of tin. It is said to be a true story.

Culloden was covered in a mist of grey; spirals of smoke from deserted camp fires curled up to meet a heavy rain-laden sky. The camps of rudely constructed branches and bracken had served as makeshift homes for the Jacobite soldiers, who had travelled hundreds of miles to face the mighty army of King George. He had a massive force of well-fed, disciplined soldiers, while the Jacobites were underfed and disciplined only by their hearts. They were a sad and hungry assortment of men and boys who had carried the banner for the Stuart crown. The ambition of Bonnie Prince Charlie to take over the throne of Britain now lay defeated, crushed and blood-spattered. It was buried forever beneath the bodies of his dead and injured followers.

High in the sky above the dead and dying, several buzzards circled over the easy prey, while sobbing kinsfolk trod softly among carnage of the battle, searching for loved ones. To witness such a sight, after embracing such a lost cause, reduced the strongest men to miserable wrecks.

On the edge of the moor, two young tinker girls were gathering firewood, when they heard moans coming from a clump of bracken. When they investigated, they found a badly injured Highlander. He had obviously crawled among the young ferns, and lay there waiting for death to end his suffering and blot out the memory of the defeat.

The girls worked quickly, each taking an arm and dragging him to the safety of their family home. When the head of the tinker tribe saw how extensive the man's injuries were, he told the girls it would have been kinder to let him die where he lay. However, in the tribe was an old healer wife who set about washing and dressing the wounds of the injured man. For well over three months she tended and cared for the Highland soldier, and thanks to her nursing skill he survived against all odds.

John McPherson, as he was called, grew stronger by the day. His Highland moor and glen, however, was under a new rule, that of King George of London, and this made him bitter and angry. All he lived for was to find his kinsmen and rise up again against the king.

News came in little snippets into the tinker encampment, and from this information he was able to see how his country was faring. It wasn't good news. The king's younger son, the Duke of Cumberland, was burning a trail through people's homes in the Highlands, seeking out followers of the Jacobite Prince and killing them. The Duke became known as the Butcher, and only the brave uttered his name in public.

John became more depressed as each day passed, with tinkers bringing in more tales of gloom and doom. One day he told the chieftain of the tinkers that he must take his leave and find his people.

'Why do you want to do this?' he was asked.

'To avenge and put right the wrongs spreading in my land.'

'How do you propose to conduct this uprising, considering that government troops are everywhere killing anyone who supports the Jacobites?'

John sat down upon a rock. His mind was in turmoil, but he felt that surely others felt the same as he did. 'I must do something, only a coward does nothing.'

The chieftain of the tinker clan joined him on the rock, and for a moment said nothing. Then he spoke. 'I have been hearing the most terrible news,' he said, 'The clan chiefs have accepted defeat and have signed a declaration of allegiance to King George. In recognition of this allegiance, land has been promised to them – vast acres. The old clan boundaries are no more. This country will never again fly a flag of her own making. From this day forth your pride is a trampled memory. It is best that you accept these changes. The authorities have also promised to stop people speaking in Gaelic and have forbidden the wearing of the tartan, so even if you manage to raise others to rebellion, they will have no colours, no natural language and no place under the new system in control of Scotland.'

Devastated by this knowledge, John ran off to find solace in remains of the ancient Caledonian pine forest which encircled the campsite. His land, his Gaelic language, his tartan were no more, but there in the forest of his ancestors he could still be a Highland Scot.

To add to his heavy burden, he pictured in his mind the low-roofed cottages of his homeland, once full of the smell of cooking bread, and surrounded by playful children, now filling the night sky with an eerie orange and red glow from the continual burning. He imagined shepherd's dogs, lost and bewildered, searching among the dead of Culloden field for their masters. In his mind's eye he saw old people left out in the cold without shelter. He was becoming more and more depressed with each vision of his destroyed homeland, until a young boy broke his train of gloomy thoughts by saying that supper was ready.

As he walked slowly back into the circle of people who had saved his wretched life, he stopped for a moment and looked at them. He counted the youths and the adults and was pleased to see how healthy they were. 'I could begin my uprising here among these tinkers,' he thought, suddenly feeling that here might lie the seed of rebellion against the government barbarians. He further thought, 'They are wise to the ways of the moors, with knowledge that the government troops don't have. There are thirty or more here, and the women, they too must possess a great knowledge of the glens and hill roads.'

His mood changed; he became filled with hope and wasted no time in sharing his thoughts with the chieftain. He wasn't having any of it, however, and told John so. John jumped angrily to his feet and shouted, 'But surely you can't allow murder and destruction to blaze around you and do nothing!'

'Why should we put our lives in danger? When did you ever think of our kind? My cousins from Nairn and Dingwall are lying dead among the hundreds of corpses on the battlefield.' He spread his hand across the place and continued, 'From this day on we shall strive for survival. We shall support no man nor defend any land. We will live at one with the earth as our ancient ancestors did. We are nobody!'

John was furious, and shouted, 'Well, I am McPherson of McPherson; my ancestors fought for this land, and if I have to wear my crest on my chest, and carry my banner single-handedly, then so be it. Tomorrow I take my leave.'

The chief faced John and said sternly, 'Listen to me now, my fine proud fellow, while I tell you who we are. When you see upon the heathery hillside our great king of the glen, the antlered monarch of the deer, he who has no foe bar man, does he have a name? The mighty eagle that soars high above his prey and hovers for ages waiting to strike, does he have a name? Where in the world is there a more cunning creature than the wily fox, does he have a name? No! Well, my fine friend, why think that you and I are better than these animals? We do not need a name, John; we are not different to the birds and animals of earth. Go and sleep on this wisdom, and then see after breakfast if you want to go and take on the might of Cumberland.'

Confused, angry and rejected, John curled under his torn plaid and fell into a troubled sleep. He hadn't lain for long when a shrill whistle broke his slumber. Word was spreading like wildfire – Cumberland's butchers were heading to the campsite! One by one the tinkers tumbled from their beds and gathered like a flock of birds around the chief. He quietened the children and ordered no one to speak unless he nodded.

A young woman came up behind John and ripped off his plaid, handing him an odd-looking pair of half-breeches. The chief whispered to him, 'Put them on now!' John had not heard the old man speak with such authority before. Pulling on the trousers and tying a leather strap around his waist, he saw, much to his horror, his tartan plaid burning furiously on the campfire.

Flames shot into the air, lighting the blood-spattered faces of the oncoming troops. They were tired and needed food. Orders came thick and fast for the tinkers to provide food and drink for over forty burly men. There wasn't even enough in the camp for three.

But before a word was uttered in reply, one of the troopers noticed John. He looked different to the others. The soldier shouted at him to step forward. John said nothing, yet he'd foreseen that this would happen, and was determined to take on all his enemies or fight to the death defending his proud clan name.

The officer in charge, a big fellow with a thick mop of red hair, walked round him, looking him up and down. He lifted a whip of thin, almost razor-sharp, leather and struck John hard across the shoulders. He flinched, but for some reason said nothing, not even giving a cry of pain. 'Who are you?' The question was spat from the soldier's thin mouth. He continued, 'Tinkers are giving Highlanders sanctuary. Has this band of vagabonds protected you? Again I demand, what is your name?'

John drew in his breath, but try as he might the words did not come. He heard in his head the reply, 'McPherson of McPherson', but his voice spoke softly: 'I am nobody.'

The chief smiled at him, but he saw that the danger was not over. If these evil men were not dealt with, death would come among his people. If the troops didn't leave soon, John, for all his pretence, would feel a sharp bayonet through his ribs.

The chief looked across at an old bent-backed woman and nodded. In a flash she reached into her apron pocket, took out some chicken bones, rattled them in her cupped hands and scattered them at the feet of the officer in charge. She pushed out a pointed chin, and in an unknown language, began to chant and mutter. A silence spread over the visitors, as they waited for their leader's response. The big red-headed man went pale. Eyes, bulging like eggs in their sockets, were fixed on the scattered bones at his feet. 'Old hag, what do you see?' he asked with quivering lips.

'A face of dread, a pool of red, dreams of demons in your head. Go from the place now, or take upon you and yours, for generations to come, the curse of the tinker!'

John was amazed at the speed with which the tyrants left. A great sigh of relief spread through the camp. Mothers gathered their little ones and went back into their tents of deerskin and rags. Two youths stayed on watch, and one by one the others, before settling down for the night, smiled and touched John on the shoulder – he was now one of them.

He later asked the old woman what her bone scattering was all about, and why had the officer run off terrified. 'Laddie, I've never yet met a red-head that wasn't superstitious.'

Next day John decided to use his strength wisely instead of recklessly. Under cover of darkness he would seek out Highland families and help them to reach safety.

Over the span of several years, he undertook many exploits with the help of his tinker family. Stories of his heroism spread across the land. From shore to shore his adventures were told with pride. No one ever discovered his true identity – he was simply known as 'The Flame among the Heather'.

11

THE HEAD

I first heard this lovely story from travellers who were staying near Comrie, Perthshire. I was fascinated by it and tried for years to find out more about it. My search led nowhere, until I was thrown a lifeline by a friend who told me it had been collected in a book. A man from the Borders called Wilson had heard gypsies tell it at a gathering round the campfire. He thought it was such a wonderful story he put it in a collection of tales.

It took me a long time, but eventually I tracked down a copy of his book. Although he had given it a different title, it was almost the same tale. In Wilson's book it's called 'The Maid of Lednick'. My version is called 'The Head'.

The story that follows is adapted from Wilson with a chunk of my own story thrown in.

At the time of the Battle of Culloden, in the beautiful Strathearn village of Comrie, lived a cotton weaver who had the same name as the village. Widower John Comrie shared his home with his lovely daughter Marion. Although he was a greedy man, known for his hard dealings with other people, he was also truthful and honest. But circumstances have a way of changing people, and our John was about to see just how much…

SOOKIN' BERRIES

Marion spent most of her time wondering along the banks of the River Lednick. She was considered a wee bit eccentric, and folks put this down to her being raised by her late granny. This old lady had filled the lassie's head with tales of the Devil's Cauldron, a swirling pool formed by a cataract of the river.

The tales Marion's granny had told her were mainly about the brownies, magical little men who lived in the area and danced around the Devil's Cauldron, and also of the 'Spirit o' Rolla', a waterfall whose voice roared like thunder in its cascading waters.

When visitors spoke of the area's beauty they spoke only of what could be seen by the eye, but to Marion the wooded valley and the high windy summits, the flowing river with its many cascading falls, held more interest and importance for her than it would for a mere lover of the view. This was her spiritual home, a little world peopled with imaginary beings, who were all her friends. Her beliefs as a child were woven like threads of gold through her youth and into womanhood. This place was her birthright; ever since those early years she had long since been embraced and enchanted by it.

If you were to sit on the edge of the basin in that mysterious glen, overhung with thick trees and shrubs, amidst the roar of falling water, you would hear the hissing, boiling, labouring Cauldron, lashed into a thousand eddies. It sounded like twisted, agonised serpents, shrieking their eternal hatred against the stream below. Add this to the noise of thunder in the heavens and many a sane person might be forgiven for thinking they had seen or heard something not of this world. In fact they might even start to believe that in the hidden caverns below lived those creatures known as brownies.

Some even went further, and said that the Devil could be heard calling on the Spirit o' Rolla to send water down for his cauldron. To those not accustomed to the place, it certainly wasn't somewhere to get lost in. Anybody of a timid disposition was likely to be terrified out of their wits!

To dreamy Marion, however, this was a world of scented blossoms and dreams. Her favourite time was autumn, not summer. The summer brought visitors, and there was less water in the stream, but when autumn with its rainstorms came to her favourite stream, she could once more hear the shrieking voice of the angry spirit as the river flooded dark and swollen.

In her wanderings in those secluded and bewitched places, Marion was generally alone, until one day her favourite cousin, Walter Comrie, began to accompany her. He was a son of a brother of her father's who had gone abroad and died, leaving a large fortune to Walter, who was placed under the charge of Marion's father, John.

It had never seemed important to her to have a friend; her secret world of imaginary creatures filled her thoughts with enough companions. Yet Walter Comrie, a handsome and well mannered young gentleman, soon became the love of her life. Seeing their constant companionship and how they held hands, it soon became apparent to all the residents of Comrie that they were sweethearts.

The people of the village would comment as the pair walked along arm in arm staring at each other with devotion, 'See how they look into each other's eyes? What a handsome pair they make! We'll be hearing the wedding bells shortly, no doubt.'

Something else was gossiped about. She was a northern lass, he a fine English gent. 'But love is a power no man can divide.' This was the reason many gave for the unusual match of a Scottish woman and English man.

Walter may have had English blood flowing through his veins, but he forgot about it when he heard rumours of the plight of the Young Pretender, Bonny Prince Charlie. Feverish stories were told of how he was the rightful heir to Scotland, and also of how mighty a Highland warrior he was. Walter had no doubts. He decided to carry the Stuart banner and join the Jacobites, the Prince's army in Scotland.

He told his lovely Marion that when the Highland troops came marching through Comrie on their way to Inverness, led by the gallant James, Duke of Perth, he would join them. Telling her was the hardest thing he had ever done. Marion was a peaceful lass, and carried no banner for any soldier's cause, regardless of who or what was being fought for. The boiling, rushing waters of the Devil's Cauldron were enough excitement for her. 'A weapon is a weapon, no matter whose hand wields it,' she'd tell anyone who was remotely interested in warfare. She would then add wisely, 'Death is death!'

It was as they sat close together watching the falling torrents at the edge of the Devil's Cauldron after a heavy rainfall that he told her of his plans.

Her answer was as he'd expected. 'What are you thinking of? You cannot leave me to go and fight a battle that has nothing to do with you! I won't hear of it.' She turned and gestured with her arms to the Spirit o' Rolla, whose voice thundered within the roaring waters. 'Do you hear this fine fellow talking of joining a Highland army, who cannot speak a word of Gaelic?' She stood up, and if he'd not pulled her back, she would almost certainly have tumbled over into the basin. She was crying and almost inconsolable, but continued pleading with him. 'And when orders are called, how will you know what they are?'

She held him tightly, sobbing deeply. 'Just because I believe in the brownies doesn't mean my heart is not flesh. Can't you see how it will break into a thousand pieces if you fail to come home to me? Stay and I will ask them to teach you songs and music. Come every day with me and we can delight in their tales. Oh please, Walter, don't go!'

Then she pushed him away from her and shouted, 'If you do go, I will ask the Rolla to send an earthquake – one that will open a passage into the brownies' underworld. They'll steal you and hide you until the battle is over.'

'Oh Marion, Marion, why don't you give up this non-sense? Your little elves may be true to you, but to me, my dear, they are nothing more than imaginings. What would the people of Comrie and Strathearn think of me, a healthy young man, wandering peacefully through these woodlands while a battle for this land rages further north? You are right, I do not speak the language of the Gaels, but my heart speaks it. And it tells me I must desert you and take up arms for the cause. I know Comrie is famous for its earthquakes and fairies, but would it not be better to be known for the fact that a mere Englishman came here and threw his weight on the side of Scotland's rightful heir?'

'I don't care a button who rules Scotland! They will have no say over flowing waters, yellow broom and weep-ing willow trees. Anyway, what if you never come back? What shall become of me? Am I to wander these places day and night, and torture myself with seeing your reflection in the Cauldron, hearing your dear voice whispering to me through the bushes? Oh please, Walter, again I beg you, don't leave me.'

But Walter had already decided that his destined path was to join James, Duke of Perth, in fighting for the scion of Scotland's ancient kings. Marion watched her lover walk off down the winding track, leaving a heart so broken at that moment of her young life that nothing would mend it, not even the magic of the brownies.

The story of Culloden is told throughout the world, and it is no secret that Walter fought gallantly. He certainly put his heart and soul into Bonny Prince Charlie's cause, but again it is no secret how that unfortunate struggle ended.

News spread throughout the land of the brave men who were now fleeing the wrath of the enemy, and many homes were opened up to hide them and assist their escape. When word reached Comrie that Walter was a survivor of the battle, all wondered how to protect their hero, especially when a proclamation was broadcast, putting a high price on his head as a traitor to the Crown. Many approached John to see if Walter needed help or a place to hide, but he said that no sign or word had so far come from the brave Englishman.

Poor Marion could neither sleep nor eat, and was in constant conversation with her brownies high up at the Cauldron on the hillside overlooking the village.

One night, not long after those events, two men, one called James Robertson and the other Malcolm Baxter, were passing by rocks that rise out of the Cauldron when they heard voices below.

'Hold him, John,' came a distinctive Highland voice which they recognised as a certain lad named Sandy Mac-Nab. 'Give me the knife and I'll do the deed. Take care of his mouth – hold his legs and watch he doesn't kick you. My, what a fuss he makes – grip him! Oh, what a tough devil he is! One of us could not have done the deed. I'm glad there's the two of us, eh, John?'

'Yes, Sandy. But look at the hole I've put in his head, and he's not dead yet!' John continued, 'He can't live long now, Sandy.'

The listeners also recognised the second killer by his voice – it was John Comrie. He could be heard hissing through clenched teeth, 'I wish it were over, for I don't like death. Look, man, he still moves! Give him another stab, but watch the blood and don't mark me with it.'

'That I will,' answered Sandy.

There was more commotion and Sandy could be heard to shout, 'Take that, you devil! I had plenty of trouble getting you this night, for you knew we were after you; but you've got it now, my fine chap, for giving us such a chase.'

The terrified listeners then heard Sandy tell John, 'He's completely dead now, so let go of his legs. He'll not speak any more of this world. Cut off his head. We will be able to take that and get what he's worth.'

'Heads these days are of some value, and this one will fetch a good price!'

'We'd better get him into the cave, Sandy, and cover him up with grass and leaves.'

The listeners would have stayed to hear more, had a female form, shimmering in a white mist, not frightened the life out of them, sending them running for their lives. To see such an apparition in the dead of night would have spooked the strongest of Comrie's weaver men, especially one that was hovering at the mouth of the devil from hell's water spout.

Once James Robertson and Malcolm Baxter were back in the village, thoughts of the murder they were positive had taken place soon filled them to bursting with anger.

'I think yon two have murdered poor brave Walter,' said Malcolm.

'I think you're right. It was clear bloodthirsty murder that we witnessed. The hand of John Comrie is at work here, my man, it's plain to see. He gets MacNab to chase Walter, catch and murder him in the coldest blood, then sends him to Perth with Walter's head to collect the reward for it. John gets his nephew's thousands, pockets all Walter's belongings, and nobody would realise he'd a hand in the death. It would be the making of the greedy bisom.'

It did not take much for this pair to conclude that this criminal deed was planned by John, because at one time each of them had been under his employment and were dismissed for theft.

They kept a watch for the return of the two so-called killers. When they appeared, a bulky parcel comfortably tucked under Sandy's arm, it was obvious that they had the head of poor Walter Comrie.

Three days later Sandy was seen striding through the village on his way to Perth, whistling happily, carrying the same bundle.

Robertson and Baxter paid a man to follow him at a distance. When he got to Perth, he was observed asking various people where the Provost lived.

Once he'd been directed to the Provost's stately mansion, it didn't take long before he stood boldly on the steps leading to the front door, the bloodied bundle secured beneath his arm. Several loud thuds on the door brought an angry Provost, asking what his visitor wanted.

'How are you this fine day, sir?' asked Sandy, bowing at the waist.

'What is it you want, lad?' inquired the Provost.

'I am here because your honour pays for Jacobite heads. Now can I please have my reward?'

The Provost cast a disapproving eye over the bloodied bundle and said, 'Whose head is it?'

Sandy puffed out his tweed-covered chest and said smugly, 'That damned rascal Walter Comrie, who fought like a lion at Culloden.'

The Provost, refusing to get too close to the bundle swathed in bandages asked, 'How can you prove to me this is the head of Walter Comrie?'

'To be sure – look, is this not a traitor's head? Did you ever see eyes like that on a loyal subject?'

The Provost, with quivering fingers, separated part of the bandages, then laughed. The object was so much disfigured that it was not possible to say even if it was a human head.

'You are a fool. Have you any witnesses to prove this is the head of young Comrie?'

'I don't think it needs proof – the thing proves itself. Take it in your hand, smell the gunpowder in it, is that not enough?'

'Listen, this is sheer nonsense. If there is no witness, there'll be no reward.'

'I am a fine honest man and I need no witness. My word to you, sir, should be my bond.'

The Provost had heard enough. He gestured at a grinning town officer who was standing nearby to throw Sandy MacNab and his foul-smelling bundle out of Perth.

'He'd better not lay a finger on me, or he'll get the same as this traitor.' With that said, Sandy put the head down on the doorstep. It rolled forward before settling at the Provost's feet. He then defiantly lifted a fist and shouted, 'Keep the reward. I can see a good man who does his duty is not welcome in the fine city of Perth.' He then turned to go, leaving the Provost and his officer lost for words.

'Hey,' called the Provost, 'take this thing with you!' In a second the head came flying through the air after Sandy like a football.

'Och, you keep it sir. Make soup for your officers' dinner.'

He seized the head again and hurled it at the Provost, then took flight as fast as his feet could shift themselves through Perth.

After the man who had followed Sandy circulated the news, the tale spread like a heather fire through the folk of Comrie. John Comrie and Sandy Macnab had murdered Walter. Sandy was going to collect a reward, while John would lay claim to the goods and fortune of the deceased man. Some reasonable people said it was a ridiculous tale, because John loved that boy – one day he would be his son-in-law, for goodness sake. However, replies were as easy to find as smoke from a windblown heather fire. Tongues were soon spreading gossip that a son-in-law was one thing, but ten thousand pounds was another. Yes, John did have a love for money, and although he loved his daughter, she was spending more and more time at the Devil's Cauldron with her elves, so how would she mind one way or the other?

The gossips were consumed with rage, and went on wildly speculating. What if this nephew of his had survived? What would happen to the respectable God-fearing weaver if the Crown soldiers were to seek him out as a collaborator with the rebels? Oh, John had plenty of reasons to dispose of his nephew, no doubt about that. Some even went as far to suggest John had become one those cursed folk who swore allegiance to the crown.

After great discussions behind closed shutters and latched doors, the conclusion of most people was that John Comrie had murdered his own nephew, on the pretext of a love for the reigning monarch, to show that he had nothing to do with Walter joining the Stuart cause.

Strathearn rang with the news. Hatred built up against John and Sandy throughout the area, and people would spit when their names were spoken. These so-called respectable individuals who lived in their midst were informers and a murderers, and crown-lickers to boot.

Soon the heather fire was spreading and a flame of hatred and revenge rose up. They were avoided; no one dealt with them; loud threats to murder them were uttered; old women cursed them with their spite for stealing the breath from Marion's beloved. In short there was no place of refuge for John and Sandy among the people of the region.

Poor Marion, she hardly could take it in – her own father a killer. But what a crime – her very own lover lost at the hand of the one who had sired and raised her. She was lost and broken-hearted. The only place she could find solace was the Cauldron. Of her father's guilt she had no doubt, because she too had been there on the night. She had heard the voices and recognised them, almost terrifying the life from Malcolm Baxter and James Robertson when she ran away, frightened and confused.

She had thought over the scene on that awful night a thousand times. She made every effort to convince herself that there must be something which, when explained, would clear up the whole sorry mess. She had also long wondered why her father never shared with her any information about Walter's fate beyond the facts known to all. Did he keep important facts from her?

Late at night she'd seen him sneaking out of the house. Once she could swear she saw someone of his build and height skulking near the Cauldron edge, but how could it be him? He hated the place, and had told her many times she was mad to go there. A turmoil of thoughts raced inside her head, offering no explanation of the awful events she had witnessed.

Deeply depressed by her fear for Walter's life and suspicion of John and Sandy's guilt, she felt that life had nothing left for her but to find solace in the brownies' dens, beside the Devil's Cauldron.

Sitting on a ledge of rock overlooking this fearful hole, she began to think more and more about how little she had to live for.

'How often have I conversed with my invisible friends in this pleasant place? How often have Walter and I laughed at the echoes of our voices as they joined together and sang of our love in the branches of laburnum hanging over the cascade of dancing waters? My heart is sore, and without love I cannot live. Find my soul, and bring me into your world, little men of the forest. Under your spells join me together again with him who was so cruelly murdered.'

She teetered over the brink, but try as she might, the courage to jump to her death failed her.

From then on Marion wandered aimlessly, reciting poetry and singing mournful ballads to her imaginary friends. The nice folk of Comrie wept for the poor lassie's broken spirit, wondering what relief could be found for the sad, unfortunate, mad girl.

Marion was just broken-hearted, however, not mad. One evening, when the moon was shining clear and bright, she tiptoed to and fro, praying and listening for one single sound that would allow her to communicate with her unseen friends. Then she heard something. From the bottom of the dell, where the water was weakest, she heard a voice. Someone was singing a low, sad song. How often had she passed this spot and thought she heard the voices of tiny magical creatures. Now they had come to her in their singing. At last she thought they were reaching out, calling for her to join them. She was riveted to the spot.

'That is not the Spirit o' Rolla, the voice is too sweet and soft,' she called out loud, hoping to get a response.

'It is not,' answered the voice. 'It's me, my lady, Sandy MacNab. Now, why don't you go away home and be with people who love you. Your father needs you and the hour is late.'

For a single moment in the midst of her misery she had thought that the brownies were contacting and communicating with her. All her life she had prayed for a word from them, but perhaps folks were right. There were no little men; she was a fool. Without a word, she hung her sad head and directed her steps homeward.

John Comrie had other things on his mind, however. All of Strathearn was baying for his blood. Thinking that if things should turn nasty it might be better for Marion if she was elsewhere, he moved her out of her home and put her under the protection of a neighbouring farmer. He thought it wiser if he too hid from sight until circumstances calmed down. In this he was right, because after he had disappeared, enraged villagers set fire to one of his properties.

Word of these matters soon reached Edinburgh and a letter was sent by the Lord Advocate commanding the Procurator Fiscal to investigate. The commanders of the Government army, anxious to quell remnants of scattered

Jacobites who might be eager to start another rebellion, weren't keen to send soldiers to Comrie, but were told it was their public duty to uphold law and order.

Walter Comrie had been murdered. If it had been because of his involvement at Culloden then that would have been acceptable to the authorities. However it seemed that the crime was committed for no other reason than evil greed on the part of the Comrie weaver named John and his companion MacNab. If the crime of murder was proven against them, then they would face the might of the law and Walter's wealth and property would be given over to the Crown, which would please the Government.

The Procurator Fiscal set about a court action. It was held in a packed church hall. Malcolm Baxter and James Robertson were examined first; and these bold lads had no hesitation in stating that they had definitely heard John and Sandy kill a man on the night in question. They were witnesses to the fact that his head was cut off, carried through the village in a bag and then taken to Perth to claim the reward.

Sandy was questioned first. 'Well, Sandy,' said the Fiscal in a serious tone, knowing how cunning and obstinate this bold lad could be, 'Is this true?'

'It is, but there's little use in speaking about the head now, when the evidence of it being Walter's is destroyed. It was the bonniest head of a traitor, when I offered it to the idiot Provost, as you could wish to see on a summer's day.'

'Aye, aye, but did you take it to Perth and request a reward?'

'I did say it was Walter's head, but the Provost called me a liar. He said it could have been anybody's head. Now that is plain, is it not?'

'Not to me, Sandy,' replied the Fiscal. He now saw that Sandy, not having got the reward, wished for some reason he could not well understand, to leave the matter in a convenient state of doubt. 'But you can surely say whether or not it was Walter Comrie's head?'

'I refused to get involved in a debate with a fine gent like the Provost of Perth by saying it was, when he said it might not be.'

'Look, Sandy, if we can't say whose head it was, then can you please tell us where you got it?

'I cannot remember where I got it. It's a long time ago, and I haven't a mind going back two days, never mind two months.'

'Well, was it off or on the body when you got it?'

'Off, to be sure.'

'So where was it before you got it?'

'On the body, where else!'

'Did you see it on the body?'

'I don't remember; but there can be no doubt that it was once on the body, so don't waste your time asking me again.'

'Where is the head now?'

'Where any dead thing should be – in the grave.'

'Who buried it?'

'The Provost of Perth, when I gave it to him with my compliments.'

'Thank you, Sandy, you can go.'

At the summing up, the unanimous decision was that Sandy was a wee bit daft, so they let him go. John, however, though he was not in court, was convicted of murder. Walter's properties were handed over to the Crown. To punish John it was decided all his properties, houses, goods etc would be put up for public auction. Of course no one would dare touch the belongings of a murderer, therefore his effects too would follow Walter's to the crown. The next step was to commit John to jail.

Throughout all these events no one gave poor broken-hearted Marion a thought. The ruin of her parent, poverty, misery and the loss of her future husband had proved too much. The clouds were ever-blackening – she had to go and find her wee brownies.

Just like the shipwrecked mariner whose eyes scanned the horizon for the sight of a sail, she hoped and prayed that the voice she had heard would sing to her once more from the Devil's Cauldron. She stood stiff and silent, and just at the same time in the evening as before, a sound of sweet singing drifted up from the chasm to fill her heart with love for the creatures of the forest.

'Oh, my dear little ones, you call me, you call me,' she cried, 'and now in my darkest hour you beckon me. Here I am. What shall I do? Open the secret passage into your world and I shall willingly join you forever.'

She waited, but nothing, no sound followed to help the maiden in her sad plight. Hours she waited, and at last, exhausted, she sat down. As her heart grew ever heavier and her spirit despaired after all that had happened, she whispered to her imaginary friends, 'You are cruel to me, for all the faith I have had in you. How many times, when at school other children made fun of me and my Walter did too, I have defended you all through my life. But look how you support me! Here I am, left alone with no one. You don't exist, I am mad! Is it not enough that my joys have been ripped from me, and now, with this flickering smoky flame of life, you take my dreams? All I had left to look forward to was to share eternity with you, my friends, yet you mock me from your mossy caves and briar bushes. Is my soul to fall upon a feather and find no resting place?'

She rose and went back home, where she found officers taking an inventory of the house and its contents. They sealed and locked every desk and drawer. A crowd had gathered to ridicule and laugh at their once trusted friend and neighbour. Many cried that he should be drowned in the Earn. Marion thought that if the mob had found him, it's certain he would have met a watery grave.

Some days later an advertisement appeared in the village, stating that John Comrie's effects were to be sold in eight days. In the village square the crowd was informed that the said Comrie had been apprehended in Crieff, and was now in Perth Jail.

That night, round a great bonfire, followers of Charles Edward Stuart danced in delight that Walter's murderer was caught. An effigy of John Comrie was then paraded and burned.

Marion sought her usual place of consolation, turning her back on bells and trumpets and the rest of the uproar. She looked back only once to see the whole village lighted up by the fire. She was going to leave everything behind to join her friends. This time she would not come back.

Far up on her ledge over the brink of the Cauldron, she whispered in desperation, 'Oh voice, I beg you to call to me for the last time.'

This time her broken spirit did hear a beautiful sound came from far below. It was not the bellow of the great Rolla cascade or the voice of Sandy MacNab, but a gentle, sweet and melodious singer. 'Sweet Marion, come and heal up the wounds of your broken spirit. Let us free your mind. Come and dance with us upon carpets of bluebell and soft-blown fern. Be our friend. We can take away the pain that the humans have so hurtfully burdened you with. Dear Marion, what harm have you ever caused anyone? Jump now, pretty lass!'

'I hear you! Yes, I'm not imagining it – you really speak to me.' She leaned over the brink of the chasm, searching the swirling waters below for the face of one of her little friends. 'The fires of Comrie are burning bright, but I know brighter lights wait for me in your palaces. Take me to your home, where there are no consuming fires, no cruel fathers, no murdered lovers, and no more unhappy days.' Saying these words she flung herself into the boiling cauldron.

Next day, all who knew Marion wept openly at the news of her suicide that was reported to them.

However, on the day before the sale of John's house and all his possessions, a commotion was heard in Comrie, greater than had ever been experienced before in the memory of that part of Strathearn. Everybody came out on the street apart from the infirm and elderly, and those indoors hung from windows with necks extended like swans. In the midst of the crowd stood none other than Walter Comrie himself, with Marion leaning on his arm, and alongside them was Sandy MacNab waving a paper above his head.

As soon as the crowd could be persuaded to quieten down for a moment, Sandy read from the paper as follows: 'This here is a pardon from the Government. It says: "A person of the name Walter Comrie of Sherrifbrae, in the county of Lanark, who took part in the late rebellion, having been outlawed, a price was set on his head by a proclamation which contained an erroneous designation of the said Walter Comrie, having described him as an inhabitant of Comrie in

Perthshire, where another person of the same name resided. Whereby the said man residing in Comrie suffered great hurt and prejudice. Therefore it is necessary to rectify the error, and to free Walter Comrie of Comrie from further disturbance." The wrong Walter Comrie was condemned, but now our Walter Comrie is a free man once again and can reclaim his property!"

When this was read, everyone embraced and kissed the two favourites, who had, as it were, come back from the grave. This joy however soon turned to shame and sorrow at the terrible way their neighbour John had been treated. 'Go to Perth and have him freed,' was the order given to two strong young men.

In no time John was entering his home village in a fine coach drawn by three good horses.

That night every prominent citizen in Comrie shared a feast in John's house, and while they were eating dinner it was apparent many had questions that needed to be answered. Mr Moodie, an old friend, was the first to ask, 'What happened? What caused the mischief, the error, the confusion? And was Walter secreted all the time in caves at the Devil's Cauldron?"

John replied that when they read the proclamation condemning Walter it was decided to hide him. Sandy and he brought him food every day. They had decided against telling Marion, she being such an eccentric lass, who might have given the game away without meaning to.

A Reverend Brown spoke next. 'But how did the story of the murder arise, and more, why did Sandy carry a head to Perth saying it was Walter's?'

'Och well,' said Sandy, 'that's plain enough. We were afraid to be seen taking meat to Walter, and thought it a better idea to give him a supply that would last him for a while. So I hunted down a young deer and left it for Walter to feed on, not knowing when John and I were wrestling with it that there were people listening to us. I wanted to take its head off to present to a gentleman trophy hunter – they're always looking for them to hang on their fine walls.'

'But what of the human head, Sandy,' asked Mrs Mactavish, a fine upstanding widow-woman of the community, 'the one you took to the Provost?'

'Well, I knew that a soldier from Glen Artney who had no relatives had died of a bad wound. So after his funeral, I waited until night before digging down into his grave and cutting off his head.'

'Oh my, that was a terrible thing to do – the poor soul!' Mrs Mactavish covered her face with a handkerchief and sniffled loudly.

Sandy smiled broadly and said, 'Missus, he was a hardy follower of the Stuarts. He'd have given his consent if he could, and I rest easy in my bed knowing that the dead soldier is not wandering around heaven seeking his head. I'm certain he's been to Perth and been rejoined with it.'

'Aye, aye,' replied Mr Moody, 'But how was Marion saved?'

For the first time Walter spoke. 'I was in the cave when Marion leapt. Her shriek terrified me. I knew the pool, having spent so long in its vicinity. I had thrown things into it and watched where they rose, every one of its eddies was known to me. When she hit the water, I knew exactly where she'd come up before she was dragged under for the last time. I succeeded in getting her onto the bank. I then took my love to the warm cave where I was hidden, and she remained there until the day that blessed proclamation was issued.'

Thus was everything explained. After the dinner a grand dance was held, in which all the citizens of Comrie took part. The festivities were enjoyed well into the next day.

Walter and Marion duly wed. She became a mother, and it was noticed that she never wandered up onto the banks of the Lednick to stare down into the Cauldron. Her belief in brownies remained firm, however, and although her husband and their children never shared those beliefs, there was something she knew which confirmed her conviction that they were there. It couldn't have been Walter who sang so sweetly and clearly on that last day when she decided to drown all her sorrows in the Devil's Cauldron – because he couldn't sing a single note!

12

A GOOD DOGGY

Here's a story about our faithful friend – the dog.

I was having a conversation one day recently in a coffee shop. My feet had had enough trekking in and out of shops with bargain displays in their windows. My companion, while hungrily munching a blueberry muffin, asked me if I believed in guardian angels.

'Of course I do,' I answered, 'don't you?'

'It's just that my mum phoned yesterday,' she said, taking another bite from her muffin, 'and she told me this story…'

'Don't talk with your mouth full,' I said, glancing at her fast disappearing cake. She apologised, and when the muffin was consumed, told me this tale.

It was in the park, where mums with babies and toddlers met mid-morning, that the big ugly dog suddenly appeared. He didn't bound around or attack other dogs, he just sat moving his head from side to side and sniffing the air. Mums kept their little ones close at hand, because this large animal had no master or walker. He was, to everyone's annoyance, a shaggy stray.

'What an ugly mutt that is – he should have been drowned at birth! Look at his big slavery, dripping jaws – and those eyes, have you ever seen such droopy eyelids like that on a

dog? What a sight. I, for one, will not let my boys near him.'
The ever-vigilant mother lifted a stick and aimed it at the
dog, shouting, 'Get out of this park, you ugly brute!'

Her companion, a little stout lady with a round face,
agreed wholeheartedly. 'Where did it come from? I'd bet
my last penny that it's escaped from the dog pound. Those
kennels are never locked properly, and that warden – well,
he's seldom sober.'

They both chatted, and as the morning lengthened were
joined by some other mothers out with their toddlers. Each
shared stories of the progress of their children, either in
running, walking and talking, or in the tender way they
looked at Daddy. Some mothers were smiling from ear to
ear because their little Johnnie had just mumbled 'Mama'.
Apart from gossiping about nothing in particular, all the rest
of the chit-chat was about the children.

All the time, from the shelter of a large evergreen bush,
the dog sat silently watching the gathering of mothers and
their children grow as the morning went on. It seemed to
be watchful about something, but no one had any idea why
such a creature had appeared in their peaceful park, or what
it wanted. One thing for sure, it wasn't welcome.

Every now and then the dog looked left, fixed its head
in that direction and stared for ages before changing over
to the right. It was obvious it had at one time belonged to
someone, but not now. For starters, its coat was too scruffy
and it didn't have a collar; every dog owner fitted a collar.

One thing for sure, the mothers were not happy about
the new addition to the park.

'I feel it only right we should report that mutt to the
dog warden. He will have to take it away. It scares me and
I can't let Freddie play on the swings in case it takes a mad

turn and attacks him,' said a tall mum, slipping off her high heeled shoes and playing with her little boy on the soft green grass which had recently been cut short. 'And another thing, what if it does a poopsy on the grass? Dog poo is full of germs. Our children will catch a disease, we really have to get rid of it.'

The rest of the mums agreed, and while two set off to inform the warden at the nearby kennels, the rest kept a wary eye on the motionless hound.

'Do you know, I think it might be lost,' said a young mum, who had a new baby in a green pram with big shiny wheels. She went on, 'Why don't we see if it is friendly? Perhaps there's a poor old gent waiting for it somewhere.' She pulled the pram brake on and sat down beside another mum on a wooden bench. As she rocked her tiny infant to sleep, she went on, 'Maybe it's the police we should inform. The dog warden will lock the animal up, and if no one claims it he'll have put it down.'

'Every now and again we get a stray wandering through,' said the other mum on the bench. 'God knows where it's from and what it's been eating, rats probably. I'm usually fond of animals, but not big ugly brutes like that. And another thing –' She was obviously not the kind of person who tolerates dogs, full stop, because she went further and said, 'My husband has an old gun, he used to go shooting when he was young. It's still in the cellar. He'll shoot the dog himself if it doesn't go away. Shoo, away, you brute!'

She stood up, flapping her arms wildly. This woke up the new-born child, whose mother abruptly told her friend to sit down, she was frightening the ducks.

In a short while the two mums who had gone to the kennels came back, saying that the warden was sober for once, and would be along shortly to catch the beast and take it away. 'This place hasn't been the same since that ugly dog arrived,' said one, looking over at the bushes, where the dog remained, still and silent.

Rocking her baby back and forth, the mother with the new born child said, 'It's only just come, and as I said earlier it might belong to an elderly person. They could be frantically searching all over for it. I think you are all becoming too hysterical about the dog.'

Just then an engine could be heard revving through the park. All eyes turned to see what it was. Along came a white van with 'Dog Patrol' printed on the side.

'Thank goodness, now we'll get rid of the beast and enjoy our visit,' said one mum with a sigh of relief. As the van approached, the dog warden called from a half-opened window to the group of mums crowding together, 'Where's the stray?'

They all pointed and shouted, but the animal didn't seem at all bothered by the noise or the warden, so it was obvious it hadn't been a stray from the kennels. 'Right you,' the man said, 'let's be having you.'

To frighten and alarm any other wandering strays, the warden revved his engine noisily. The van gave a roar, lunged forward, and then, to everyone's utter horror, it gathered speed, heading straight for the pram with the new baby. The child's mother had been talking to a friend, and had moved away from the pram momentarily.

'Help!' she screamed, 'my baby, my baby!'

There was no way the out of control vehicle could be halted – the baby faced certain death. But the instant before the van collided with the peacefully sleeping child, the big ugly dog leapt through the terrified crowd and knocked the pram out of the vehicle's way. With no care for its own safety, the shaggy animal protected the tiny infant with its body.

The van, with the drunken warden at the wheel, careered down an embankment and landed in the pond, scattering ducks and swans, in a cloud of feathers, skywards. Several agile policemen wasted no time in pulling the driver from the crashed vehicle and breathalysing him before carting him off. No doubt he'd be facing the future without a job or driving licence after that escapade.

When the commotion had quietened down and statements been taken from all the witnesses, everyone was praising the hero of the day. They wanted to pat and hug the big dog, their fear and disgust now gone. But much to their disappointment, there was no sign of the dog – when the mother took her baby in her arms, it had simply disappeared. The other mothers and the police searched everywhere, but not knowing the dog's name, they couldn't call for it.

Next day, before anyone else was in the park, a very grateful mum came back with a bag of tasty doggy bites to say her own special thank you, but the big dog was nowhere to be seen, nor did anyone ever set eyes on it again.

Was the strange dog without an owner a guardian angel, waiting there to protect the baby? Or had it just taken fright and run off? Why was it there in the first place? All these questions remained unanswered, and it is likely that is how they will remain.

I have a feeling a certain baby will grow up being told the story of what happened on the day a strange dog suddenly arrived in the park.

13

THE DEVIL'S HELPER

Here's another story from the Chapman's book.

Two hundred years ago, there lived a farmer by the name of Rab Allan in the Monklands district near the town of Airdrie. His farm had a reputation like no other. It was known for hundreds of miles around that he employed a woman named Maggie Ramsay, who could gather, stack and build haystacks faster than anyone else.

So good was she at her job that Rab began to take bets on her. He'd have competitions in haystacking to see who could finish the job first. Lots of harvesters from Stirling, Perthshire and the Borders, who thought of themselves as champions at gathering time, crowded onto his land near the Auld Burn to lay bets. But no matter how good they believed they were, Maggie always cut, stacked and finished her hay faster than anyone else.

News spread all the way to the Highlands; to a place where left-handed Sandy lived. Word reached his ears that, in Monklands, a woman wore the reaper's crown. Up until then, Sandy thought he could not be beaten. He was the very elite of the Highland haystackers. He had to meet and challenge this person.

Now Sandy possessed another gift; he had the second sight. If there happened to be any form of cheating in the competition, then he'd know about it.

He spread word among the crofters that he'd heard about this Maggie Ramsay, and was heading south to meet up at her farm and challenge her. Did anyone wish to accompany him? Well, in an hour he was standing on the road facing south, with over a hundred fellow crofters by his side, all eager to see the contest and maybe to get a wee bet at the same time.

It took near a week to reach Rab Allan's farm, but after a night's sleep and some belly-filling porridge, Sandy was ready for the fight. His scythe, sharpened like a razor, was ready in his hand.

'Come now, Rab, and bring forth your champion. I have money to bet – aye, and so have these hardy lads who have come with me.'

When Rab saw how much money was being flashed about, his heart leapt with glee. 'Maggie, come and meet your opposition,' he called out.

It was the half-moon shaped blade that appeared first, held tightly by a small hand. But, oh dear, where was the big giant of a woman everyone imagined Maggie to be? Here was a skinny wee thing of maybe five feet tall, with small feet and not a muscle to be seen. If anything, Maggie looked undernourished.

'What kind of a trick is this you're playing, Rab Allan?' asked Sandy, adding, 'Is there half a dozen Maggies hiding in the corn?'

'No, Sandy, this is my lassie, and if you have any doubt

as to her capability, then feel free to start work at the same spot as she does.'

'That's a good idea, because I want to watch this woman work.' He slowly paced around, eyeing her from head to toe. If she'd a cheating way of working, he'd sense it.

In due time both opponents stood in the middle of the field. She'd work to the right, he to the left. It was eight o clock in the morning. Rab held a greyish rag in the air and waved it. 'Begin,' he commanded.

A huge sigh went up as Maggie, head down, began her expert work. Sandy threw himself into his. Down the field she went, swishing and cutting; Sandy sliced through his part of the field. Up and down they went, on and on.

After several hard hours' graft, Sandy straightened his back and took a breather. He felt confident. Then his eyes near popped from their sockets when he saw that not only had Maggie cut twice as much as he had, but she had stacked it as well. His friends, who had begun the contest shouting in support and cheering him on to win, were strangely silent. Like Sandy they were in awe at Maggie's speed. Her feet didn't seem to touch the ground.

Sandy suddenly felt that all was not as it should be. He closed his eyes and silently called up the spirit of his ancestors, who arrived in the form of a light breeze. It blew gently among the remaining corn in the field. He stooped down, and far off on the far side of the field he saw the moving feet of Maggie as she rushed up and down. But as he looked closer, with the aid of second sight, something caught his eye. Maggie didn't have feet at all, what he saw was two hooves, the feet of a goat!

Taking his scythe with him, he crawled speedily through the corn towards Maggie. When he reached her he stood up and asked her to stop work. When she turned to face him Sandy almost fell backwards, because it wasn't the little woman he'd challenged earlier to a harvesting competition, but a demon, complete with green face, jaggy teeth and pointed horns.

Sandy lifted his scythe above his head and swished it down upon Maggie, the creature of the devil. She leapt high up above the corn, screeching and howling. As all eyes watched, the demon whirled around Sandy like a hurricane. He closed his eyes and gave one last stroke of his blade. A howl ran across the Auld Burn, over the rooftops of Monklands and up into the September air. In a puff of red mist Maggie disappeared, leaving Sandy shaking in fear.

Maggie wasn't the only one to vanish. Rab Allan, who it was later discovered had been seen on several occasions at the midnight hour sitting on a rock at the Auld Burn, conversing with a hooded man, took his leave. People who had bet on Maggie lost their money, but Sandy went home with his reaper's crown firmly back where it belonged.

His famous story of how he beat a fiery demon was told repeatedly, until tractors and combine harvesters were invented, putting an end to champion reapers, left-handed or otherwise.

14

THE BOORAK TREE

This next tale is modern, but its roots reach back into the mists of time. There is no documented evidence of how the ancient Picts lived in Scotland long before the Romans arrived, which happened about two thousand years ago. My people, the travellers, tell stories that have been handed down through the generations and some have stayed vivid despite the passing of time. This next tale I share with you may have originated in the time of the ancient Picts, but then again, maybe not.

Make sure the doors and windows are locked, because this is a creepy tale…

Mary was tired. She had been working most of the day tidying up autumn leaves, piling them high and burning them up in heaps. She was well prepared for the winter frosts and snow when they would come to cover the earth.

She eagerly enjoyed her tea and biscuits afterwards, but now she had a chore far more important than garden cleaning. It was Halloween, and soon the pattering feet of guisers would be heard in the street, and there would be giggling and laughing as they called on all the house dwellers to 'trick or treat'.

SOOKIN' BERRIES

Harry, Mary's husband of fifty years, had died two years ago. It had always been him who got over-excited about the Halloween visitors with their eager, painted faces – happy children, dancing with excitement.

But Mary had as a young girl listened fearfully to tales of the hallowed eve, when ghosts and spirits drew near to the living; a time of shadows and dreams. These tales were told to her by her grandmother, a cold-hearted, frighteningly dark individual whose stories were anything but joyous. Today the festival was looked on as nothing more than a time for playing games and dressing up. However, in Mary's early years the opposite was the case. To her Halloween meant a night without sleep, a time when fear spread through all children who were reared with legendary tales handed down from Pictish times.

Her granny, and the generations before her, had upheld the ancient ways of a culture long since dead to all but a few, her granny being one of them. Halloween had a far deeper meaning to the old ones. Harry had laughed many times at Mary when she said it was a time, not for celebration, but for an all-night vigil to watch over children and protect them from evil.

Harry was no longer around, but a lifetime of keeping to his view of the night and not hers was to be continued. If she had fears, then she certainly wasn't going to allow them to appear.

Seven o'clock rang out on her old grandmother clock as she busied herself filling saucers with sweeties, nuts and biscuits. The children would come with their painted faces, reciting poetry and singing songs. She enjoyed their young company, and when the knocks came welcomed them at the door.

Just as she was running a comb through her short grey hair, the phone rang. It was her friend from the library, young Anna. Weekly they'd meet for coffee and chat about their day to day lives. The conversation was mainly taken up with stories of Anna's two children, nine-year-old Egan and Andrew, aged seven.

'Hello Anna,' said Mary, 'what is it?'

'Oh, the most awful thing has happened – Mummy has had a heart attack!'

'My dear girl, that is terrible! She's not… I mean how bad is it?'

'Doctor says, if she pulls through the night, then she has a good chance of surviving. Mary, I have to be with her.'

'Of course, Anna, you must be at her side.'

'Will you come and stay overnight with the boys? My husband is offshore on an oil rig and cannot possibly make it home. Please say you'll help.'

Mary felt a cold shiver run up her spine. She and Harry had never had children of their own. She'd no knowledge of how they behaved, what they ate and oh my, no, she didn't want to be responsible for someone else's children. But how could she not do it? Anna, faced with a very sick mum, had no one else to turn to. The family had only been in the town for a few months. Mary was the only person Anna knew and trusted.

She heard herself say the words before she had time to think more about them. 'I'll be there shortly.'

'The taxi will be with you in ten minutes!'

Mary closed her curtains, climbed the stairs, switched off her electric blanket and pulled plugs from their sockets. Just as her hand turned the key in her back door, the horn of a taxi was heard outside. Slipping on a green wool coat and hat to match, she smiled and apologised to a line of skeleton-clad kids bounding up to her door shouting 'Trick or treat, Mary!'

'I have to go away tonight, boys and girls, but if you come to visit next week I have lots of sweets and fruit to give you.'

Their sad faces and sighs of disappointment made her feel like the greedy giant who hated children. However a task of great importance lay ahead – two boys whom she'd never met, called Egan and Andrew.

When she arrived at Anna's house, Mary instinctively took some money from her purse, and through the half-open glass partition offered to pay for her fare. Her driver waved a hand and said, 'No need for payment, missus, the fare's been taken care of. Oh look, here's the lady going to the airport.'

Anna was already rushing down the stone steps, her small overnight bag swinging from her hand. Fastening the last button on her coat, she kissed Mary's cheek and said, 'I'll phone as soon as I get there. And boys,' she turned to the pair of wide-eyed children, 'Make sure Mary has everything she needs.' With a banging of car doors and revving of engines Anna was gone, leaving a breathless old woman whispering to herself, 'Life these days is too fast paced for me.'

Introductions on doorsteps were not to her liking either, 'Now let me see, you are taller, so you must be Andrew, the older boy. Let's go inside.'

As the door closed a mumbled answer came, 'Uh ah,' followed by, 'he's Egan.'

Inside, Mary was pleased to see a warm, glowing fire. Although it was electric, it was nevertheless a cosy sight on the last day of October. A large settee with lots of knee rugs and scatter-cushions beckoned her to slip off her shoes and coat and sit down.

But no sooner had she laid down her coat when, to her utter shock and horror, the kitchen door burst open and out bounded a scruffy black and white collie dog. Within seconds Mary's legs and ankles were licked all over. 'Shush, away with you, you daft dog!' Her coat went back on quicker than it had come off. Anna had not mentioned this extra responsibility. Maybe if Mary had known about it she'd not have agreed to come. The boys were laughing loudly at both the look on her face and the dog's.

Andrew spoke first. 'Maggie won't bother you, and she's a softy.' The dog rolled over on her back, all four legs to the ceiling, tongue hanging from a panting mouth. 'See,' said Andrew, 'she'd not hurt a fly.'

'She needs to be walked,' whispered Egan, nudging his brother in the ribs. 'In all the rush, Mummy forgot to take her.'

This little fellow was obviously shy, so saying nothing to Mary, he ran into the kitchen and came out with Maggie's collar and lead.

'It's only a short walk in the woods behind our house,' he said, standing by the door. 'It will only take minutes for her to do her business.' Already he and Andrew were donning anoraks and woollen hats.

'Just hold on, you two, there are lots of guisers out tonight, and some are letting off fireworks. What if she takes fright and runs off? Mummy will be furious with me for losing her dog.' Mary was already making excuses, but the boys with Maggie on the lead had unlocked the back door, and before she could stop them were running into a thick copse of trees.

'My goodness, its pitch black out here,' she said, calling them to come back. But as they took her by the hand and rushed her almost off her feet, it was clear they had other ideas about obeying. 'Oh dearie me, slow down,' she gasped, trying to catch her breath.

They let go and walked beside her. She squinted her eyes, and could just about make out tree shapes with orange street lights behind them. In their midst something caught her eye. Looming among the shadows stood a thing from her past: twisted and gnarled, with knotted and warted trunk, it was a Boorak tree.

Her Granny had told her of such a tree – a soul gatherer, she called it. Suddenly, she saw in her mind's eye the old woman's face as she narrated to her how evildoers from Pictish times were punished. They would be tied securely to the trunk of a Boorak with their throats cut and left to bleed to death. Into the tree trunk, kept there forever, went the evil that had come out of them. Afterwards the criminals' bodies were burned and scattered back over the earth.

In those days there were no policemen to uphold laws or jails to hold prisoners. Long ago, before religion and before books, punishment for crimes was administered at once. It all happened thousands of years ago, but Mary's granny believed in the old ways. As Mary stood there before the tree in the dark wood, she heard in her head her old granny saying, 'Never interfere with the Boorak!'

What happened next would have sent Granny running for her life if she was alive: Maggie leapt at the tree and broke off a branch.

'Bad dog, drop that! Now, I say!' Maggie had other ideas for her stick, and was already running around shaking it. Mary's shouting frightened the boys. They reached out to each other and held hands. In an instant she composed herself; after all, she was a stranger, they hardly knew her.

'Sorry, boys I'm not used to dogs, or to young men come to think of it.' No way should she let her secret fear upset them. Calling quietly to Maggie, she suggested they go home. After all, Halloween was no time to be wandering about in woods thinking about evil trees or anything else.

Back inside the warm, cosy house, she scolded herself for being so stupid. Maggie, with her stick, had retreated to a wicker basket full of squeaky toys and ripped teddies. The kettle whistled gently, and after the boys had replaced jerseys and trousers with pyjamas, the threesome settled on the comfy settee to drink milky cocoa and sugary tea in front of the dancing red flames of the electric fire.

Mary laughed at their jokes, with a solemn promise not to tell mummy the naughty ones. Then she did what she did best – tell stories that her granny had shared with her. Not, however, the Boorak tale. Eleven o'clock struck loudly on the carriage clock on the mantlepiece; time for bed. The boys were good company, and she began to wish that she'd been a mother. 'Goodnight, you two, and remember no playing on your computer thingys.'

Andrew pushed past his younger brother, causing the little lad to lose his balance and fall backwards. Egan jumped up and thumped his brother on the back. Mary scolded both of them. Then she did a last check of the doors and windows, making doubly certain she'd switched off the cooker at the main socket. After a final check of the plugs in the kitchen, she patted the dog, flicked off the light and closed the door behind her. She quickly looked round the sitting room, then headed for bed.

She'd barely begun to climb the stairs when a cold shiver

ran through her bones, prompting her to think, 'Someone is standing on my grave.' What a strange saying that is – and not a bit relevant, just a silly old-fashioned remark. But it happened again, then twice more. She felt cold, and pulled a wool shawl tightly round her shoulders with one hand, steadying herself on the banister with the other.

At her next step she stopped dead. A form stood at the top of the stairs, a faceless floating apparition. Her hair rose up at the base of her neck. 'What is going on?' she asked herself. Suddenly the door of the boy's bedroom swung open, and Andrew, who was holding a wire coat hanger tied to two brush handles with a white sheet draped over the home made contraption, called menacingly, 'Oohhh!'

This made Mary furious. She was not in the least bit amused, and when she reached the bedroom gave him a right rollicking. 'I'm an old lady and could have had a heart attack on those stairs. You are very naughty. Wait till I tell your mum.'

Egan rushed over and patted Mary's hand, saying, 'I told him not to do that, Mary.'

'Huh, it was only a joke,' said Andrew, half apologising.

But Mary had already calmed down, and feeling the tension and anger subside, she turned away her head, plopped out her false teeth, turned to face him and made the most horrible toothless grimace. Both of the boys dived into the room and under their bedcovers. Smiling, she closed their door and said loudly, 'Only joking!'

As she slipped under her own bedcovers in a cosy single bed in the spare room, she could hear loud laughter coming from next door. Obviously they'd seen the joke.

A romantic novel with a bookmark lay by her bed on a cabinet beside a soft night light. After reading a short chapter her eyes began to flicker shut. Peace seemed to reign in the boy's room and she too fell asleep, content and relieved that she had managed to carry out the responsibilities which had been forced on her that day.

Sometime during the night she awakened to the sound of voices. At first she thought the boys were up to more tricks, so she said nothing. When a cold bat-like creature fluttered above her head, she chuckled in amusement. Sitting up, she switched on the lamp, about to make another toothless grimace, but then she saw that there had been no mischievous prank from her charges. The room was empty!

She fumbled for her glasses. Nervously scanning the small room, she whispered, 'Who's there?' This seemed senseless, because it was easy to see there was no one there. Her sleepy eyes darted into every dark corner as she felt for the satin bed quilt. But to her utter horror, an invisible hand was already pulling it slowly off the bed.

Unable to grasp what was happening, Mary thought that perhaps all the responsibility of the night, the dog incident and being away from home had given her a nightmare. Yes, that's it – she was living a dream. She closed her eyes tightly, and for a moment sat on the edge of the bed. She opened them again expecting to see a normal bedroom scene, but when she did, it was no dream! Her sheepskin slippers floated out from beneath the bed and hovered in mid air, while all the time the voices whispered. The curtains waved back and forth, and the ceiling light went on and off by itself.

To her utter horror, shadows were dancing on the walls, long arms waving back and forth. Shivers went up and down the entire length of her spine. As she watched the shadows growing from floor to ceiling, her heart began to beat like a thudding drum in her chest.

The menacing voices grew louder; it was time to get out of there. Beneath her feet dead twigs crackled; she was wading through mounds of fallen dried leaves, not the shaggy pile of carpet. Reaching for the door handle, she was grabbed by two long and spindly hands that stretched out to her from the shadows. Those voices grew deeper, moaning and calling, 'Give it back, give it back!' Up till then the voices had made no sense, just mumbling unintelligibly.

'What do you want and who are you?' Her throat felt dry and the words seemed to stick there. She coughed and said loudly, 'I have two little boys in this house. I beg you not to harm them.'

Silence followed as the shadows faded into the walls. The long thin arms fell into the floor of autumn leaves and broken twigs. Outside an owl's hunting cry was a welcome sound after the haunting of her bedroom.

Mary repeated her question and waited. A rustle on the floor, like a rabbit scurrying over leaves, rooted her to the spot.

A tree began to grow in front of her, not in the usual sense of sprouting but like it was some kind of creature. Mary felt her strength being sapped from her into the dark greenish brown trunk with its slimy bark. It grew larger and wider until half the bedroom was full. Concealed in the trunk were dozens of faces; faces of horrendous, twisted, evil-looking people with eyes staring at her. This was where the whispering had come from, those foul faces. Every one screamed at Mary, 'Give it back!' over and over again.

She covered her ears and closed her eyes. 'What do I have to give back?' As her eyes flickered shut, she fought hard to stop herself from being sucked into the trunk with all those demonic faces. 'Please, tell me what it is I have.'

A force of immense power pushed her against the bedroom wall, bringing a sense, not of fear, but relief that the tree wasn't stealing her body. A deep growling voice said, 'Look at the top of the tree.'

Lifting her head upwards, she froze at the sight of Andrew and little Egan. 'Oh no, not the children!' She pleaded with the demon, whoever he was, to let the boys go and to take her instead. The boys seemed to be asleep, resting among the tree's branches. That was one cause of relief. Mary clasped her hands together as if in prayer, and begged for the boys to be freed, but all the voices continued to scream, 'Give it back!' over and over again until she could take no more.

Feeling for the door handle at her back she turned it, and in a moment stood shaking behind the closed door. Tears rolled down her cheeks. She was completely helpless, and as she stood there a whimpering sound came from the bottom of the stairs. It was Maggie the dog.

Mary turned on the stair light and called on the dog to come up. It was just a dog, but at that moment, it was the only friend she had in the world. Suddenly, as the dog edged upwards, her mind raced back to the walk in the woods and a certain stick. The Boorak tree's broken branch. That was what they were asking for, of course!

'Maggie fetch!' She grabbed the banister and moved as fast as she could down the stairs. 'Come on now, who's a good girl? You are. Pretty Maggie, fetch the stick.' The dog's head bobbed from side to side and looked stupidly at her. 'Blasted animal,' she shouted, and tore downstairs and into the kitchen, grabbing the dog's ripped teddies and throwing her squeaky toys in the air. 'Oh no, there's no sign of the thing,' she cried, fearing the worst.

In a fit of anger she kicked the basket, forgetting that her feet were bare. That made matters worse, so with all her strength she threw the dog's bedding and basket across the kitchen floor. Lo and behold, as it hit the washing machine, what should fall from under a torn rug in the basket – the very branch itself!

In seconds, ignoring her swollen arthritic knee joints, she was bounding back upstairs again. Faltering for a moment, she prayed the boys would be alright. She opened the door, closed her eyes and pushed the branch into the shadows. A chill ran through her bones as a slimy hand covered hers for a moment. Then the voices fell silent, and a warm air replaced the freezing cold that had previously filled every inch of the house.

Mary didn't feel at all courageous, just terrified that whatever this was, it had come into the house on Halloween night, the night when spirits are closest to the living, and that it might have taken the children away. The thought didn't bear thinking about, so she opened her eyes in the hope that her two charges were either sleeping on her bed or would be found standing in the room. Neither was the case. She could see nothing but two discarded sheepskin slippers, lying awkwardly on the shag pile carpet next to her dishevelled bed. 'Andrew, Egan,' she called, 'where are you?'

'We're in here!' came the answer from next door, a response which to her was as sweet as honey.

Rushing in, she found them lying there undisturbed and completely dozy. 'What's the matter, Mary?' asked little Egan, sitting up in bed and rubbing his sleepy eyes.

She was astounded to see that neither boy had been disturbed. They had seen no tree or ghosts or shadows or branches; nothing. 'I heard a scraping noise,' she lied.

'Oh, that'll be Maggie wanting to sleep on your bed,'

answered Andrew, refusing to emerge from under his football-patterned duvet.

Mary apologised for waking them, and whispered as she closed their door, 'I'll let her sleep on my bed, seeing as it's just for the one night.'

Sleep was the last thing she wanted to find, and she spent the rest of the night downstairs in front of a busy telly with the sound turned down.

If she had thought that the Boorak tree, with its spirits, had ever been a figment of her late grandmother's imagination, then from that night onwards old Mary knew just how real it was.

15

FROZEN BOOTS

This next tale has been a favourite of mine for over fifty years. I have shared it with children from Australia, Ireland, Wales, England and most of Scotland.

It's about a piper named Sandy; a gentleman of the road who, as this story begins, found himself penniless and freezing cold in a storm on the last night of the year. Come on the road with him and see how his future was shaped by a dead man's boots.

Sandy shivered from his hunched shoulders to his split-soled boots. Winter's jaws were snapping and barking at his exposed heels as the north wind signalled an oncoming blizzard.

That year, as he'd done for most of his adult life, he had accompanied the drovers who herded many hundreds of Highland cattle from the island of Skye to the cattle market in Crieff. But never before had the beasts fetched such rock-bottom prices. Paying his men and laying aside next year's cattle fund, the drove master was left with as bare a purse as he'd ever had. Poor Sandy was handed only a few pennies, with apologies and promises that the price of meat might be higher next year.

So there he was, with a paper-thin plaid, boots unable to keep out the fingers of Jack Frost, his toes turning blue with cold. Oh, he was in a terrible state right enough, but he was alive, and while the heart was beating, old Sandy kept up his hopes. It was Hogmanay, the last night of the year. It was a time for first footing, and who better to bring in the New Year in Scotland's glens than a hardy piper?

At the mercy of the first gale-driven snow, Sandy saw a welcome sight. Far up on the hillside was a flickering light. Through the blizzard which was tearing like a raging bull into every corner of the land, he could dimly make out the low roof of a small croft. Warmth spread through him as he thought of the welcome that lay within that small house.

The light was still quite far away, and the storm was battering him hard, so he decided to rest for a minute behind a hedge of beech that stretched along one side of the road. As he pulled his threadbare plaid across his thin frame and curled his shaking knees up under his chin, he suddenly became acutely aware of the presence of another person. Sandy called out, to reassure whoever it was who was sharing his shelter. In case the person was up to no good, he assured the stranger he had no money or belongings worth stealing, so the best thing was just to say hello and be done with it. But his words remained unanswered.

Apart from the wind howling and a chorus of rustling dead beech leaves whirling around his head, no voice spoke in reply. Twice, three times he called out, so certain was he that someone else besides himself witnessed the mighty storm in the dark, while the devil danced a fearsome jig among gust-driven snow.

Now, Sandy wasn't one to admit he was wrong. He felt the ground on either side of where he sat, shivering with cold. To the left, he touched stones, heather clumps and stumpy hedge roots – nothing. To the right, he repeated the process – but what was that: leather heels, he felt two boots! Running his hands along the boots he drew back in horror. The footwear was being worn by somebody. There were feet inside the boots, and legs above the feet. Oh no!

This was no person, however. Well, maybe at one time it had been, but now it was a corpse, dead as a dodo. Sandy apologised silently for disturbing the man's last rest and quickly left the shelter of the bush.

However, when his feet sank into several inches of fresh snow and the chill sent him rigid, he became a desperate man. Desperate men do desperate things. Those boots with their toes pointing upwards were going nowhere; their master had no need of them. Boots, as Sandy saw it, are for living men, not dead ones. He must have them!

Going back, he felt under the hedge for the boots and tugged at them, but they were not for leaving their owner. Again and again he heaved and pulled, but they were frozen solid. The only way for the piper to get his new footwear was to cut them free. 'Well, there's a first time for everything,' he thought, as he drew his dirk and wasted no time hacking off the boots – feet included.

From that moment, Sandy had only one thought in mind, to get away from there as fast as he could go. With the wind at his back, he had no problem making his way swiftly up the hill, towards what he was certain would be dinner and a wee dram to warm his innards.

Soon he was standing where the glow from the croft window shone its welcome light into the darkness and driving snow. He felt its warmth; at last he'd arrived. His Glengarry tammy and plaid were white with snow, but with a quick flick and shake he was ready to share Hogmanay and party away the night with the good folk of the house. He rapped at the door.

When the woman of the place saw him on her doorstep, however, she refused to allow him to set a foot in her home. She was adamant that she never allowed his kind over her threshold. No matter how much he begged and pleaded, it made no difference; she held firm at her doorstep, with the howling gale nearly drowning out her voice. Her husband joined her and looked Sandy up and down. At last he said, 'He's a simple piper. He's harmless enough. Let him sleep out the storm in the barn.'

'You heard him,' said the woman. 'Now, take yourself away into the barn, and remember – in these parts we rise early, so make certain you're gone when we get up.' These words and a slammed door told him there would be no food or dram for him to bring in that New Year. Never mind, he was alive, and maybe in the morning someone would give him a bit of bread to fill his empty belly.

Whistling blasts of freezing wind filled the barn with sounds of doom, and had it not been for the friendly old cow munching away in a trough full of oats he'd have been totally miserable. 'Hello, old lady,' he said, removing his tammy and bowing stiffly. 'I hope you won't mind if I sleep here in your grand mansion this bleak night.'

The cow continued chewing, unmoved by his presence. Her face had no leer of murder about it, unlike that of her mistress, who would no doubt prove a woman of her word if she found him there in the morning. Another pleasing sight was the hot steam coming from the cow's nostrils – just the thing for defrosting frozen feet. Sandy wasted no time in plonking the dead man's boots, feet and all, into the cow's trough, and making himself a bed in the straw for the night.

Exhausted, he fell into a deep sleep, not moving a muscle until the cock crowed for the new dawn. Swiftly removing strands of straw from his clothes, the piper looked inside the cow's trough. Her warm breath through the night had certainly done the job. The boots, with bones, blood and dead flesh intact, had completely defrosted.

In no time the piper had the gory feet removed and the boots on. Brilliant, he thought, they fitted like gloves. Never had he owned such well-made boots. They were of calf leather, part-laced with strong metal eyelets. 'That poor soul, whoever he was, hadn't had much wear from these grand boots,' he said to himself, walking up and down the length of the barn.

As the thought of dead man flashed into his head, he felt uneasy. 'What if he's on his way to heaven and him without feet? I know, I'll give him my old boots. He can come up to this barn as a ghost and be joined again with his feet before journeying to the mansion in the sky.' No sooner said than done. He put the dead feet into his old worn out boots.

The next moment, the sound of a door slamming filled him with horror. It could only be the man or woman of the house, coming to see if he had overstayed his welcome. There was no time to escape, so he hid again in his bed of straw and prayed that whoever it was didn't have a gun!

From the sound of the feet in the cobbled courtyard it was the woman who was coming to the barn. He listened intently, keeping perfectly still. The footsteps came into the barn and then stopped. For a moment there was no sound at all. Just when he thought she'd found the place empty and gone off, there was an almighty scream. Her husband heard her and came rushing to her aid. 'My dear,' he said, sounding deeply shocked, 'I thought for an awful minute that piper chap had attacked you!'

'That piper chap?' She stared at him with as furrowed a brow as he'd ever seen on his wife's rugged face, 'He'll never bother anyone again. See there in the trough, your mad cow has eaten him!'

When the master saw what was lying in the feed trough, he scolded the cow for eating a smelly old piper.

'You must bury him, husband,' ordered the farmer's wife. 'Our good neighbours will be here today, and if so much as a hair is found, they'll suspect foul play. Now, do as I say, and get those bones and boots buried!'

Reluctantly the man took the pair of boots and their contents down to the bottom of the garden and proceeded to dig a hole, watched all the while by his nagging wife.

Back in the barn, Sandy had decided enough was enough. His belly was not only empty but dry as well. He needed to be fed and watered. This couple, she with her cutting tongue, he a snivelling coward, were provoking this desperate piper to commit another reckless crime. Into his mouth went the untuned chanter, a weapon to be reckoned with, even though certain folk hadn't got respect for the national instrument of old Scotia. With all his remaining strength the piper filled the bag with air and pushed into it with bony elbows. A screech, not unlike that of the ancient banshee washing funeral shrouds in a lonely fog-covered river, rent the air.

All that remains to tell is that the farmer and his wife ran off as fast over the hill as if the devil himself was after them, scattering white snow in their wake, and they have never been seen again – not so much as the tip of a nose. As for our hero – well, he's got himself a fine wee croft with a warm bed and as much food as will last him a long, long time. Oh yes, and not forgetting the cow, with her milk, butter and full fat cheese. He's a happy man indeed.

If you find yourself facing the last night of the year when a blizzard is howling through your street, remember Sandy!

16

THE CRUEL MILLER

This is another tale which I've shared throughout the land; it teaches bullies how not to behave. I hope you enjoy it. My dear friend Robert Dawson gave it to me. He informs me that he got it from travelling people.

Old Tizzy and her son Jack lived alone on a remote moorland some place in England. Jack made dolly pegs, paper flowers, baskets and brooms and Tizzy sold them. They were saving to buy a horse and wagon so that they could move away from there and go on the road. Jack's dad had died the previous year, and since his death they'd found life much more difficult. It was such hard work carrying baskets, hawking from door to door, that Tizzy's fingers grew stiff and painful. One day Jack said, 'Mother, I will get a job.'

'Oh son, I'm sure that's a very admirable thing to say, but getting a job is harder than you think.'

'Why mother? I'm strong and healthy, with good eyesight and can work all day long on only a plate of meal.'

'Dear son, you're a traveller boy. Nobody would trust you.'

'Well, if I don't try, then I will never know.'

He decided that after breakfast he'd go down into the nearest town and ask around to see if anyone needed a strong lad.

Butcher Brown was slicing chunks of beef when Jack enquired about work. He was delighted when the butcher looked him up and down and said, 'Lift that pig's carcass, sit it on your shoulder and show me how far you can carry it.'

He was very impressed with Jack when he saw how fast he worked and offered him a job. However when Jack told him he lived in a tent on the moor with his mother, the butcher said abruptly, 'Sorry, I don't employ travellers.'

Sadly young Jack walked off, until he came to a busy baker's shop. The same thing happened there – he was offered a job, but when he said how he lived, he was turned away. Onto the next place, and it was the same story, they did not employ travellers.

Jack felt terrible; he couldn't understand why people didn't like his kind. After hours without any success, he stopped to rest on the outskirts of the town beside a large house with lots of windows and a big red door. After a while a tall man came out, leading another man by the hand. 'Hello,' said the tall man to Jack, 'nice day.'

'Yes, but I think it will be wet,' he answered, feeling spits of rain on his face.

'Mary,' the tall man called back through the half open door where a tiny lady stood. 'It's going to rain.'

She walked back into the house and came out seconds later with a basket. 'Thank you, Tom.'

'It wasn't me, it was this young man here who says it's going to rain.'

'Thank you, young man,' Mary the tiny lady called out,

as she hurried out to the washing green and gathered laundry off the line.

Jack smiled as Tom and his companion came over to him. 'This is Bill, he's blind,' he told Jack. Both men held out their hands. Jack shook each in turn, introducing himself. They invited him to share some lunch with them. He gladly accepted, and when in the house met Mary, who had been born with rickets, leaving her with deformed legs. She told him she had difficulty walking, but did the best she could. Along with Tom, Bill and Mary there was another man called Roger who couldn't remember things. Tom was deaf but very good at lip reading.

Jack spent the rest of the day with his new friends, who all lived together looking after themselves. They even grew their own corn. 'You are such kind people,' he told them as he got ready to go home. 'I'll visit you when I come back to the village looking for a job.'

Mary looked at her friends and said, 'The miller needs someone.'

Bill, Tom and Roger said in unison, 'Oh Mary, that would not be fair on Jack.'

Jack's ears pricked up, and he asked what the miller did that was so wrong. He was simply told that the miller wasn't a nice man.

His new friends refused to say any more, because they relied on the miller to grind their corn. Without the mill, they'd have no bread.

Jack assured them that travelling people are used to being treated unfairly. A job would mean money and a better life for Tizzy. So having said farewell, he set off with the directions to the mill in his head, and soon was knocking on the mill door.

'I'm a strong lad who needs a job. I won't let you down. I shall be here every day when the cock crows and leave as it roosts. Give me a job and you will not regret it.'

The miller turned Jack around and examined his muscles. Jack felt as if he was a horse for sale.

'Be here at six o'clock tomorrow morning. I'll give you a trial period, and at the first sign of laziness, illness or cheek you're out the door, is that clear?'

Jack felt good as he ran off to tell Tizzy the good news – he had a job!

He left his campsite just as the sun was peeping over the horizon, and soon stood eager to take up his post as a miller's apprentice. This sounded quite a title, but as day followed day it became all too clear that the young man did all the lifting and carrying, while his boss lay around doing nothing but shout orders. Jack hardly had time to eat his lunch, when every minute he was humping two heavy sacks of grain at a time up the long narrow steps to the threshing mill.

When the miller wasn't trotting orders off his tongue, he did something else – he made fun of Jack's tent and his traveller culture. But every week, for all his hard work he was paid a wage. This he proudly took home to his mother, who saved it in a leather pouch. One day that horse and wagon would be theirs, and they would be able to take the road again as all travellers long to do.

For all the constant name-calling, young Jack felt no ill-will towards the miller and refused to let his taunts bother him. After all, sticks and stones might break his bones, but words could never harm him.

Then one day, when the main milling season had begun, who should come to the mill with a barrowload of corn? None other than Tom, the tall man from the house on the edge of town with the red door. Jack rushed downstairs to carry Tom's corn up for milling, but the miller shouted at him not to. Tom would do it himself. 'Come on now, Tom, bring that corn up here,' the miller whispered.

'He's deaf and won't hear you. The best thing is to stand in front of him so he can read your lips,' said Jack, pleased to help his friend. The miller sharply reminded him that Tom came every year, and he knew exactly how to treat him.

Standing in front of Tom, the miller covered his mouth and sang mockingly, 'Tom, Tom, tell me dear, who has stolen your floppy ear? Can't say who or can't say when, turn around, come back again.'

Poor Tom repeatedly asked the miller what it was he was saying, because his hearing had became worse in the past year. Jack was furious, so he took Tom's bag of corn and told him that he'd have the flour ready for him next day. The miller shouted at Jack, accusing him of spoiling his fun.

Next day it was blind Bill's turn. He was pushing his barrow of corn with a white stick in his hand, and when the miller saw him he said, 'Three blind mice, see how they run, eating Bill's corn and having fun.'

Jack heard this and said, 'Hello, Bill, is it your corn you want milled?'

Bill felt for Jack's hand, saying, 'Many thanks, Jack. It's good to know you're here.'

Taking hold of Bill's sack of corn, Jack trudged upstairs with it. The miller shouted after him that if he spoiled his fun again, then he'd be sacked

Next day, Roger came to the mill and the same thing happened. The horrible miller made fun of him too. 'Roger the dodger, can't think right, sleeps in the day and works in the night.'

What a shame to see Roger standing there crying, because the miller had confused and upset him. Jack gave him Bill's flour to take away as he'd done with Tom's.

Next day it was tiny Mary's turn. She could hardly push her barrow up the steps as she had been told to do by the miller. When she eventually got to the top he laughed and told her to take it back down, and then up again. 'The grand old Duke of York, he had ten thousand men, he marched them up to the top of the hill and he marched them down again, hee hee. Mary has no legs, just a pair of twisted pegs, she's too small to throw a ball, what a fool is she, hee hee.'

Although he had been ordered not to help anyone again, Jack couldn't stand by and watch such dreadful treatment. He told Mary to collect Roger's flour and leave her load with him. 'I'll bring it to the house tomorrow,' he told her.

The miller was furious, and tore strips off Jack for spoiling his annual fun. Jack told him it wasn't right to poke fun at people who couldn't help being different. The angry miller replied that it wasn't his fault they were cripples, and anyway, what harm did it do. Jack said nothing else. He thought he had better work twice as hard, or the miller might sack him.

That night, though as he shared supper with Tizzy, she asked why he'd been so quiet lately. When he told her that the miller was a cruel man because of the way he'd treated his friends, people with special needs, she smiled, patted his hand and said, 'That miller needs to be taught a lesson!'

After supper, Tizzy put her plan into motion. The first thing she did was to sow a miniature pair of bellows into the hem of her long coat. Then, in an inner pocket of her coat she deposited handfuls of river grit. She also hid a kettle iron in another concealed pocket. The last thing to be hidden away was a piece of wood about ten inches long.

Jack was astounded to see her do this, and even when they went to bed for the night he had no idea what his mother was planning.

At breakfast he found that she had risen an hour before him. 'Now, son,' she said, 'I will take your place today. The miller will think that you are sick. I will tell him that I'll do your work for half a day, because no doubt you'll be there in the afternoon when you're feeling better.'

'But mother, I'm not ill.'

'Of course not, but the miller doesn't know that. Listen, now what I want you to do is to go to the house with the red door and bring everyone to the mill at exactly twelve noon. The cruel miller will have learned his lesson by then.'

Jack knew the ways of his mother, and smiled as he watched her head off towards the mill. That foolish man had no idea what Tizzy had up her sleeve to cure him once and for all of his bad behaviour.

'Hello, miller, I'm Jack's mother. He's not well today, but frightened that he might lose his job if he's not here to do it. I'll fill his boots until he comes in at twelve. He assures me he'll be feeling better by then.'

The miller laughed at the sight of the small, thin woman and said, 'I need bags carried up those steps which are heavier than you.' But Tizzy had carried heavier loads than those bags, so putting her shoulder under one, she heaved it up the stairs without any problem.

The miller was impressed. He showed her what the job was, then left her to it. As he went into his office, she called out to him, 'Will I see the ghost? I'm not staying a minute in this place if it appears to me. Folk in these parts have told me this place is haunted.' She watched as the miller stopped dead in his tracks. He turned around with a puzzled look on his face. 'That's the first time I've heard rubbish like that,' he said.

'Oh, I've been told many times about the boy who floats around in the flour dust. People say that he can do all kinds of damage to the working wheels and threshing machinery.' She could easily see her words were taken in by the miller. He was no fool, though, and so he laughed off her tale of woe. He strode into his office and slammed the door. It was then that Tizzy began her haunting of the mill. First, she threw a handful of river grit into the grinding wheels. The noise was dreadful: crit, grut, hork, prrrrittttit. She heard the miller's door open, so threw in a little more grit. 'Miller,' she screamed, 'what is that noise?'

He rushed into the threshing room and listened to the awful din. 'I don't know what it is, I've never heard the like of it.' He stood and waited until the grit had travelled through the wheels and they sounded normal once more. Just as he was about leave, Tizzy pushed her heel down on the tiny bellows sown in her coat hem. Instantly, clouds of white dust floated upwards, giving an unearthly shape in the air. 'Help,' Tizzy screamed again, sending shivers down the miller's spine. 'What is that?'

Not waiting to find out, the miller ran off into his office and slammed the door. Tizzy followed on his heels. 'Miller, you assured me that no haunting would take place in this building. But me being of the gypsy blood, I can feel that there is a ghost. Did you hear the awful sounds and see the ghostly dusts of flour?' Before he could answer, she continued. 'Butcher Brown told me the cause of it was the miller before you. He bullied his young helper. The poor lad couldn't stand the treatment he got, so he threw himself into the wheels. Oh miller, do you think he's back to haunt us?'

Again she searched his face for fear. It wasn't long in coming, 'I had nothing to do with that. Why would he haunt me?'

Tizzy turned the door handle and said, 'Do you know of anyone who taunts those less fortunate than himself?'

He lied, and said no he didn't. Then, composing himself, he ordered her to get back to work. Tizzy obeyed, but instead of going upstairs she slipped downstairs and put the piece of wood between the machines that separated husk from corn. This meant that the bags were filled with husks instead of corn – the worst thing that could possibly happen to a miller. She then ran upstairs and dropped more river grit into the machinery.

'Miller,' she screamed yet again, 'listen to the noise, and what on earth is going on downstairs?'

He rushed out of his office, with the gritting and crunching going on from the stones upstairs, and went downstairs to find a chaos of husks bagged and corn spilling everywhere.

'What is happening?' he shouted, rushing into the room where Tizzy was blowing eerie clouds of flour from her hem, drip-feeding river grit into the millstones and looking very afraid. 'Is he here?' asked the miller. She'd taken the opportunity to rub flour on her cheeks as she stood shivering amid the madness of the mill, and answered, 'Listen, miller, if the working of this place stops we will know the ghost has come back. But the question is, is he seeking revenge?'

The miller was terrified and shaking with fear as he grabbed her arm. 'Please don't let him get me! I don't mean what I do, it's just harmless fun.'

Tizzy pretended not to know what he meant. The miller was a coward. Most bullies are. She calmed him, and said, 'It might be that the ghost has gone. You go and put the kettle on, and I'll finish my morning work.'

It was almost twelve o'clock as she put the final touch to her plan. When he'd gone off, she took the heavy kettle iron and dropped it into the machinery. There was a crunching sound which could be heard for miles. 'Miller,' Tizzy really was acting now, 'he's here for you!'

'No, don't let him take me!' The miller left his office and was bounding downstairs when Tizzy halted him. 'Wait, miller!' she called, 'he'll find you no matter where you hide. What has to be done is for you to make an apology to the people who you have wronged. Only that will stop the ghost from stealing your soul!'

At that precise moment, coming up the road were Bill, Tom, Mary, Roger and Jack. The miller rushed up to them, shaking their hands, apologising repeatedly and swearing that from then on he'd be of exemplary behaviour. While this was taking place, Tizzy slipped away unseen.

From that day on, the cruel miller was known throughout the land as a gentleman; he was good to deal with and as fair a tradesman as anyone knew for miles. Jack's wages were doubled and his workload halved. Never again would people deal with the miller without a handshake and a smile.

I think in England today there's an old lady with her son who travel the back roads and byways in as fine a wagon as ever there is, drawn by a thoroughbred piebald horse.

17

DAVIE BOY AND THE DEVIL

Here is another Chapman tale. Time and place have no meaning for the characters of our tale, so let's just say it happened a while ago, in this place and that.

Davie was a traveller boy who had, after many years, come wearily home from a seafaring life. On his return he was looking for his family. When he at last arrived at the camp-site where he'd last seen them, he was sad to see it deserted, empty of old and young, with not even a dog or pony.

Sitting down on a stone, head in hand, he looked around the place where so many children had played and he felt heart-heavy. Scanning the site one last time before heading off, he noticed that where his tent usually stood was a mound of earth, perhaps only a foot wide. As he began to scrape away small handfuls from this mound, he recalled his father saying to him as a little boy, 'If I have a message for you, I'll bury it.'

And yes, this was a message from his father, because in the hollow he had dug lay a box. In it were three biscuits and a note. The note read: 'If you be hungry, my son, don't eat these biscuits until you have shared them.'

What a strange thing for his father to say, he thought. Still, his father was a wise man, and he had taken the time to conceal the box for Davie, who by the way was beginning to feel quite hungry. However, he would abstain from touching a morsel until he met somebody hungrier than himself.

This opportunity was just around the corner, because there he found an old bent-backed woman who asked him for a small crumb of food.

'I only have three biscuits, old wife,' he told her, 'but you are welcome to share one with me.'

The wizened wife thanked him, ate the half biscuit and went away at a snail's pace.

Soon he came upon another old lady and she too asked him for food. 'There are only two biscuits in my bag,' he said, 'but I'll share one with you.' Again the elderly soul thanked him for his kindness and tottered off.

Two days later, his hunger had taken on a life of its own, and was gnawing at his innards. 'I must eat this last biscuit,' he thought in desperation, scanning the skyline in the hope that someone would appear. Just as he was putting the biscuit to his lips, a voice from the roadside reached his ears. 'Help me, please, I am starving to death!'

Davie made over to a patch of rough grass to find, lying in a dreadful state, another ancient woman. This one was even sicklier than the others.

'Help me to sit up, young man,' she begged, 'I have no strength in these bones.' Davie bent down and gently seated her at the foot of a tree trunk.

'Here, old wife, I have only one biscuit left, but you can have it all.'

'Thank you, my good man,' she said, handing him a woven sack. 'You deserve much more than a biscuit.'

Davie thought the old woman was perhaps losing her marbles, for what good was an empty sack to one who was in the last throes of hunger?

'When I am gone down that road, you open the sack and ask it for whatever you desire, but never for a thing of badness or greed.'

Those parting words left Davie totally confused. He scratched his head and sat down upon the same patch of grass that the old woman had sat on no more than minutes before. The hunger returned with a vengeance, eating steadily deep into his gut. He peered inside the sack, and making sure no one should see him and think his actions were those of a madman, whispered, 'Can I please have food?'

And had he food? Did he ever! For there, to astonish his eyes, was a table bigger than one set in a banqueting hall, laden with every kind of eatable one could wish for. For someone who only had the merest crumbs of shared biscuits in his belly, was that not a feast! Davie ate until the last bite swelled in his throat and nearly choked the once hungry lad.

Then he lay down among the sun-warmed grass and slept like a baby – he slept and dreamed of steak and vegetables, puddings and creams, salmon and fruits, all produced from his old hessian sack. Yes, if ever there was a happy traveller man, then he'd be hard pushed to be more pleased than Davie.

Awakening much refreshed, he carefully folded the magic sack and tied it over his shoulder. Little knowing or caring where his wandering footsteps would lead him, Davie set off down the road that led to somewhere or nowhere.

By the day's end he'd arrived at a town nestled within high stone walls, in the middle of which was a castle. 'This is a strange place,' he thought, noticing that there did not seem to be a single inhabitant.

As he looked all over for a place to shelter for the night, it soon became apparent that not one of the houses had a light or open shutters. Finding no one to ask about this, he went and knocked loudly at the castle gate. He waited some time, before at last the gate creaked open, and standing peering out from behind the heavy wooden gate was an old man who asked Davie his business.

'I need digs for the night, where can I lodge?'

The elderly man told Davie that he would find nothing in this place, because the Ancient One had eaten most of the people. The rest had taken to the hills, in fear that they too would be feasted upon.

'The Ancient One,' asked our traveller lad, 'and who might he be? And can he not eat food like the rest of us?'

The old man was rather taken aback by Davie's response, and asked him where he had been for the last ten years and more. After realising Davie had been away on the high seas, the old man beckoned to him to come in and share his supper. Davie didn't feel the need for food, having eaten enough to choke a horse, but thought it best not to offend the man and said a drink of tea would be fine.

They drank down tea and then Davie discovered what had been happening to the people of that place. He drew on his pipe, did the old man, stared into the fire and began. 'One night, when Her Majesty the Queen was alone in her chambers, she made a wish that the King's dungeon would be filled crammed full of gold.

Suddenly she turned to see a tiny man dancing in the flames of her fireplace. He said that if she wanted her wish to come true, then she had to bring two handmaidens over to the fire for his master. Without question, the greedy monarch did as he asked.

The most terrible thing happened next. A dozen little men, just like the first, grabbed the two innocent maidens and drew them into the fire, never to be seen again.'

He went on to tell how the King, on hearing this, was horrified at the evil greed of his wife, scolding her for dealing with the underworld. She said that, before he judged her, should they not see if the tiny man had kept his part of the bargain. So down into the dungeon they went, and yes, there it was, a mountain of sun-coloured gold filled every corner.

But the King was not impressed, and went into his wife's chamber to see if the magic forces could be summoned. At once the little man appeared to him and said, if he wanted things to be as they used to be, then he must bring the Queen over to the fire. This he did, and in an instant she too was seized and swallowed up by the fiery imps.

Then the rooms began to shake. Flames shot forth from the fire to curl and slither up the wall. The fireplace was glowing like a furnace. Then the master of all terror, of all horror, and in the most grotesque form, the Devil himself, shot out and held the King by the throat. 'You will bring me and mine food – living, screaming, kicking food! Do you hear me, mortal?'

The quivering King nodded his head vigorously. The Devil, as suddenly as he had come, was gone, leaving a cold fireplace and a wreck of a king.

'So now you see where the townsfolk have gone,' the old man concluded.

Davie thought long and hard before saying that he might be able to help. He asked to see the King. After climbing several flights of winding stairs, the pair were ushered in to sit before a bent-backed and sad-faced man. He was not old, yet he had the appearance of one who had lived a dreadful existence.

'I have a young man here who thinks he may be of assistance, your eminence, sire,' said Davie's companion, with a note of despair in his croaky voice. The king hardly lifted his head to look at Davie, but bade him to sit anyway.

Davie told him that he too had a powerful magic, one not to be used for greed or evil but only for deeds of goodness.

'Take him away to do what he wishes,' said the King to his faithful old servant, though neither of them had the slightest belief in the help offered by Davie, or anyone else for that matter.

Davie was taken into the royal chambers, and soon had the fire kindled, spreading a warming yet menacing heat throughout the room. He didn't have long to wait before the tiny man he had heard of came flickering over the flames.

'Have you food for my master?' he enquired.

'Yes, I have,' answered Davie.

'Then give it here,' squealed the demon.

Davie shook his head several times before saying he had to see the Ancient One first. The last word had no sooner left his mouth when the ruler of demons whooshed up from the fire and hovered in the room like a tower of solid flame. Davie felt his toes curl inside his boots and his tongue swell with fear.

'Where is my meal?' roared the earth-shattering one. 'I need to be fed!'

'Sire, I have a meal better than any living, scrawny person – would you like to taste it?' Before the Devil could do to him what he'd done to all the other mortals, Davie spread his sack on the floor, peered inside and summoned it to produce its best. It did not disappoint: the whole room began to fill with every possible edible morsel.

'Come, eat, fill yourselves up,' the Devil called to the demons, who were pushing and shoving to be able to feast upon Davie's gifts. The Devil was the first to gorge himself, spewing and slavering his way through fruits, beef stews, fishes and fry ups, until not a single crumb was left.

The Ancient One liked these new delights, and ordered Davie to be there again the next night. Davie came again as he was told, and the next night also. After a week, when he was certain he'd gained the trust of the king of the demons, he set about his plan.

'Keep all the doors open leading from the chambers and down the stairs, and also open the castle gate,' he told the old guard. 'This night we will see the end of the Ancient One and his family of gargoyles. Trust me, old man.'

That evening, as usual, when the fire was lit those wicked vipers from the pits of Hell came forth to feast. With drooling, slavery lips they waited impatiently, scratching at Davie and then at the sack. The Devil ordered Davie to produce food, or else they'd eat him instead.

'Now, listen here, you lot,' said the bold hero, 'why do you wait night after night for a feasting, when you can enjoy the pleasures of the sack all the time?'

'Well, tell us more, then, Davie boy, please come closer and tell us more.' The Devil pushed aside his family of ghouls in anticipation, curling long fiendish fingers round Davie's neck.

'It's easy, my lord of the underworld – jump inside!' The drooling band gathered in a tight circle and peered inside the sack. 'I see nothing,' said one. 'Nor I,' hissed another.

'Of course you can't see anything, because you must all jump deep inside. Only then can the sack work its magic.'

Davie felt the Devil's bony fingers loosen their grasp as he bent down to sniff and peer into the blackness of the sack. His followers, waiting for his orders, gathered round.

'Let's try this, my wiry little worshippers,' the Devil cried, then leapt into the sack. In an instant the rest of his band did the same. Davie waited until the last cloven foot had disappeared from view before whipping a strong length of rope around the opening.

'Look out,' he screamed, 'I'm coming through, I've got the Devil on my back!'

Out of the room and down the stairs he darted, with the bag of Hell on his back. Out through the main door, out through the courtyard, out through the castle gate, on to the street he ran and ran, with all the demons of hell scraping and screaming on his shoulders. The King, who had heard the commotion, was standing on his castle wall shouting from the high turrets, 'Haste on, Davie, haste on my man, you'll do it!' His old guard was leaping and dancing in the air, cloth hat whirling above his head.

Davie went round the bend in the cobbled street, and with one last dash began emptying Hell's cargo down into the town well. Down, down, they went, tumbling and rolling and screeching, never to escape the blessed water of the well again.

Davie had used his sack as was asked of him by the old sick lady – 'Never ask for anything out of greed, only need!' Well, folks, if ever a sack was used for need, then it certainly was this one.

Before long, word spread that the Devil was defeated, and soon the townsfolk came from where they had been hiding back to their houses. The King began to do his duty, and soon found a worthier Queen than the last one. And as for brave Davie, well, one day while washing at a quiet river, he met and was reunited with his family and never needed to ask his magic sack for anything again. He kept it safe, however, just in case.

18

I CAN FLY

It has been great fun recording the old stories for you, and I hope we do it again in another book soon. To finish off I want to share a few real-life stories from my past as a traveller. Remember at the beginning of the book I told you about my life on the road in a big blue bus? Well, come on back to those old days, take the journey with me.

This is what I did at the tender age of six...

It was a beautiful warm summer, and we had met up with some relatives in Crieff, Perthshire. Our campsite, on the low Comrie road, was at one time a Prisoner of War camp. During World War Two there were four very large POW camps in Scotland. When the war ended, some prisoners from Germany and Italy liked Scotland so much they stayed on and spent the rest of their lives there.

As the camp was built by the Army to accommodate hundreds of prisoners, it meant there were toilets already there, or lavvies as we called them (I shall bring these into the story soon), and a supply of fresh water. There were solid concrete bases to keep our bus home on, and this meant

Mum didn't have muddy welly boots dirtying her carpets, another bonus.

In the year I write about, several families joined ours, and for a long summer we played at ghosties and hide and seek in the thick yellow broom, which grew in abundance along the river Earn's banks and up to the doors of our mobile homes. We enjoyed cutting branches of broom and making brushes. Our parents allowed us to sell our home-made brushes to neighbouring farmers. When we had sold enough to give our mums money to help pay for school uniforms, we spent the rest of our earnings on sweets and ice-cream when we went to the Saturday movie matinees.

So there we were queuing up along with lots of Crieff kids waiting for the Ritz picture house to open. Crushing through the doors and rushing inside to see our favourite weekly serial added to the excitement of the day.

This particular Saturday, the serial was just the most brilliant story of a flying gent called Batman. When I sat down on the big cloth seats in front of the massive screen, bag of sweeties firmly grasped in my tiny hand, I wanted time to stand still. No one could tell me that there weren't a hundred musicians hidden behind that screen playing their very hearts out as Batman flew from the highest skyscrapers. I was transported.

Afterwards I couldn't even remember walking home the two miles from the Ritz, down the High Street, along King Street and past the Gallows Hill, where only a hundred years ago, real life outlaws hung by the neck until dead. Nothing distracted me from my imaginary life in the clouds with the greatest hero of all time, Batman.

After the film I could hardly think of anything else. 'Mum, Dad, guess what?'

'What?' they both said, looking up from their news-papers.

'If I was dropped from a great height, would I fly to safety?'

'Away, lassie and don't be stupid. If I'm not mistaken, wings are needed to do that.'

'Batman does it!' I screeched in reply. 'He flies all over Gotham City.'

Dad smiled, folded his newspaper and said, 'There's no such place, lass. Batman has kid-on wings made of Hollywood leather strapped to his back, the rest is done with camera tricks. Now be content with those legs of yours and be grateful they work. Wings are for birds. Off you go and play.'

As I kicked at stones and twigs in my angry and dejected state, all I could think of was my hero, saving maidens from burning buildings, or catching baddies and throwing them in jail for robbing banks. No, Batman had real wings, how else would he be able to save the world? I would prove to my parents that, just like bats and birds, us humans can fly; nae bother!

However, on *terra firma* I could only get to about three skips and two jumps – I had to get up on a high roof to start with, that would be the only way to use my wings. Oh, I couldn't feel any sprouting under my shoulder-blades, but I was convinced that as my chin was launched into the wind they'd appear like magic and I'd soar upwards.

Cousin Anna and other traveller kids were playing over by the lavvy, and as I ran to join them, something monu-mental loomed on my horizon – the lavvy roof. What a brilliant take-off point, a perfect sloping roof from where with a few swoops I'd be airborne.

I called on cousin Anna and the others to starting building steps to the roof with a few boulders that were scattered around. In no time they had completed a fairly stable set of stone stairs.

'Why do you need this?' they asked. Promptly, and with much pride, I told them my plan. This started up a chorus of, 'Silly fool, away and no be so daft. You'll flatten the broom when you plummet to the ground – and wait till your mammy finds out!'

Well, I informed them that nothing ever happens if clever folk don't take the lead, or something like that, and proceeded to climb the steps. I later found out that I was ten feet from the ground. It felt good surveying the caravans and our bus roof, and for the first time I realised that rivers from a height look like giant snakes. Truth be told, I began to feel slightly sick and decided maybe humans couldn't fly after all. Batman might have been scared too, but with that mask on you didn't notice his face.

I was about to abort the take-off, when suddenly, beneath me, a laddie who was doing his business on the toilet let out a loud resounding fart. It was the last thing I remember as off I flew from the roof.

From then on it was a hectic dash from examination by a doctor to the emergency department of the hospital. I lay in Dad's van cursing every inch of Batman, the invincible. Little did I realise at that point that my right leg was broken in five places.

When I came to after the operation to reset my leg, I was tucked up in a white-sheeted hospital bed being waited on by pleasant ladies called nurses. There I stayed for six weeks. No more flying for me!

19

A NATURAL LOVE

*This is a lovely warming story of when my sister Janey discovered
her natural love – horses.*

Early June in Oban was a favourite time and place for
travellers, we loved it there. No surprise, then, to find us
camped not far from her lovely beaches. Mum's brother had
settled there many years before, so whenever we found our
road stopping in Oban, Mum visited our uncle Charlie and
swapped family joys and tragedies.

We had other reasons to enjoy that part of the west coast.
The beaches had bonny pale sands, untouched by debris,
seaweed or rocks. Bare feet were at home on the Oban
seaside. If the weather was warm we'd play all day, catching
the incoming tide in freshly dug pools to float paper boats
in, or simply to bob up and down in ourselves, depending
on how deep we had dug. Sandcastles became whole villages. Then, tiring of building, we'd swim in the Atlantic
water until we resembled wrinkly prunes. We didn't have
a care in the world. Our childhood was filled with such
heavenly places.

That particular summer my sister Janey, who was five years older than me, found her natural love, one which was to stay with her for life.

In a field near where we had camped was a beautiful stallion, a big horse about twenty hands high. Jet black like midnight without a moon, he was the bonniest beast she'd ever set eyes on in all her sixteen years. She loved horses. Daddy knew if there were any nearby then that's where she would be. She had a way with them; she would whisper in their ears, and could make them do her bidding without any difficulty.

After a few days she asked Dad who owned the horse. He knew that his daughter would ask him that question, so he'd found out earlier from a factor on the estate which bordered the field. The horse was a surprise birthday gift for the landowner's daughter, who was due home soon from university.

Dad warned her to forget about the horse. He didn't want her upsetting any landowners or factors. Janey said she'd only look at the animal from the gate and not approach it. But as it turned out, she would find this impossible.

That night it was hot and clammy. Janey found sleep difficult. She pulled on my pyjama collar, asking, 'Are you sleeping?' I told her I was, and she should do the same.

'I have something to tell you,' she whispered. I told her that if she didn't shoosht, Mum and Dad would wake up and not be too pleased. She leaned over and whispered in my ear, 'I can ride the horse. I was on it bareback today. But keep it secret.'

'Dad will go crazy if he finds out,' I told her. 'Leave the beast alone, it's not yours and never will be. Anyway, he's a stallion and you know how unpredictable they can be. He will love you one minute, kick you to death the next,'

'He's a big cuddly teddy bear, and he loves me to bits. My face is raw with him licking it.'

Next day she asked me to go with her to see the landlord; perhaps he would let her ride the horse. He was a nice gentleman and took Janey into the stables. He obviously recognised and respected her natural interest in horses. He told her, though, that the stallion needed a lot of manhandling before he was ready to be ridden, and she'd be wise not to approach him.

The sun was exceptionally hot when we arrived home. I helped Mum with the dishes as Janey rabbited on about the stables. I wriggled into my red swimming cossie, still damp and full of sand from the day before, and chased after the big breakers rolling onto the beach. My older sisters, who'd been baking in the sun, were the colour of chocolate. The early evening brought supper alfresco.

Later, as the day headed to its close, we went to bed, leaving Janey whispering in the stallion's lug. Dad doused the fire, calling to her to come to bed. I think he was hoping the animal would either give her a sharp kick or bite which would put paid to her horse interest. He wasn't too worried though, because he knew that after tomorrow we'd be gone from there and she'd have to find a new friend. It was berry time, and the long journey from Oban to Blairgowrie meant an early rise for us all.

All was in its place and peaceful when suddenly Babsy, the youngest of our family, sat up in bed and said that Janey wasn't in hers.

Dad was furious, and said, 'She'll be in the field yapping with the stupid big horse. I warned her to stop her nonsense.' He pulled on his trousers, pushed feet wearily into his boots and went outside.

For a wee while we didn't hear a thing, then he came back and whispered to us to come out and see something. Like a row of little skittles we lined up beside the bus. He pointed at the beach – and what a fantastic sight was before us. Janey could be seen riding flat out as the stallion tore along the sand at full gallop. Horse and rider were one as they emerged into a blaze of black and orange, silhouetted against the red horizon.

Our Janey had known that come morning she'd have to say goodbye, so she had stolen her only chance. The stallion wasn't dangerous; he needed human contact and Janey gave it. Both would find another road in their lives, but that night, with the setting sun disappearing from view, and the picture of my big sister and her friend, will live in my memory forever.

My sister from then on made sure that horses would be her life. For a long time she ran a horse sanctuary, taking in sick animals and providing warm stables and food until their lives ended.

20

TINY

I'd like to tell you now about how we acquired our first pet, a very small fox terrier aptly named Tiny. It was berry time, and we had all arrived on our campsite, Ponfads, on the outskirts of Rattray and Blairgowrie.

It all happened like this...

When coming into the campsite, I noticed, as we drove past in our bus home, a bow-shaped camp at the far end of the green. A grand fire was blazing away, and round an old woman nearby played three of the reddest-haired children I'd ever seen. No way would their mother misplace her kids with flame-red hair like that.

After putting the basin on its tripod outside the bus door for washing hands, I skipped off to play. 'Don't you lot go too far,' Mum reminded us as we shot off to explore. 'It'll be suppertime as soon as I get the stovies done.'

The thought of a nice big plate of steaming hot tatties, onions and corned beef made me call back, 'The hunger's on me, so don't worry, I'll be playing round the door.'

I was curious, though, and leaving my sisters playing in safe view, I went to have a look at the bowed camp with the red-headed kids.

This was the type of abode my parents lived in as youngsters, and it always held a fascination for me. The construction itself was an art handed down from father to son. With Scottish winters being so severe, there was no room for errors in putting it together. If rain and draughts were allowed under those canvas shelters, then new-born babies and elderly parents would certainly suffer.

They were built like skin around a ribcage. Animal skins were used originally, and these were later replaced by jute sacks, plastic sheeting or tarpaulin. Hazel sticks, formed into bows while the saplings were still young, became the skeleton for those nomadic homes. When the time came to move on, it was a simple matter of removing the cover and untying the sticks, which were all held together with a ridge pole, and piling them neatly onto a cart. Usually a small horse pulled the cart around the countryside. However, if there was no horse, the entire contents of the travellers' lives were distributed onto their own sturdy backs.

To add to the comfort of the tents, water was drained away by digging a shallow ditch at either side, allowing water to run freely away from the floor. In winter, heavy stones were used to stop strong winds blowing the cover off and away. Ropes were also used as extra security. Where two canvases joined, usually in the middle, a wee stove was used to give heating and cooking. This was a lifesaver in the cold winters Scotland was at one time accustomed to. A long chimney (lum) was pushed through the roof to take away the smoke.

Relatives told me of the ghost stories they heard as children during winter nights while huddled inside, with gales and blizzards swirling round their cosy home of long ago.

Now, getting back to the tale…

'Hello,' I called over to the children sitting beside the old woman. They were shy wee things, and as I got nearer, they couried their faces into the elderly woman's chest.

'Hello to you,' said a voice from inside the camp. At that a younger woman pushed her head out, and, deary me, she too had blazing red hair.

'My children are afraid of strangers,' she told me.

'I'm not going to hurt you,' I assured them.

The old lady smiled but didn't look at me; instead she asked if that was my bus she saw trundling onto the green. I proudly said it was. She told me they always relied on Bonny, their horse, to take them where they needed to go, but she had died a week ago.

I looked around and saw horse tack laid across a nearby tree, which had been on the animal that had brought them to the berries. I asked who had taken away the carcass. She pulled her shawl over her head and said nothing. I was thinking it strange that there was no man in the group, and being a youngster, I asked where the head of the family was.

'We're from Argyllshire. This is the first time we came to the berries,' said the younger woman, brushing her long red hair as she stooped coming out of her camp. 'This is my mother, Bella, and these besoms are my children. Clara is the oldest, she's six. Rory here is a big four, aren't you my laddie? And Florrie, my baby, is three. The berry farmer kindly removed Bonny for us. Poor old thing, she was over thirty. The dear creature was glad to go, I'm certain, but Mum loved her so much, she's still mourning her passing.'

Then the woman freely told me that her husband Ronald had taken very sick and he too was gone. A tear slid down her cheek. I felt guilty at my nosiness and immediately apologised. Then I quickly changed the subject. 'Oh,

I love animals too, but we're not allowed any in case they run under the bus and get squashed.'

I turned to speak to the little ones. 'I bet you can't guess this, but I have seven sisters!' Ice broken, the kids took to me straight away. I was fascinated by their hair colour. I wanted to take them to our pitch and show them to my parents and sisters. 'Can I take them up to meet my wee sisters?' I asked, adding that I was called Jess.

'No, lass,' said Bella, 'it's nearing their bedtime. Tomorrow morning you're welcome back.' That said, she crawled into her tent.

'See you in the morning then, Jess,' said the children's mother, who told me her name was Isa. They waved goodbye, as one by one they followed granny into the camp for the night.

As I was leaving, Bella called to me, 'Would you like to have a peep at my dog's new born pups?'

Given my love of animals I didn't need inviting twice. The old lady gently lifted back the doorflap to display a tender sight. Lying curled up beside their mother were four of the smallest puppies I'd ever seen.

'My goodness, how small they are,' was all I could say.

'The old dog is nearing her end,' whispered Isa. 'You know she's had a lot of litters in her life, but I fear this last one will kill her.'

The poor old dog did look fairly peched, and didn't bat an eyelid when I lifted up the nearest pup, a black and white ball of fluff. But this one didn't catch my attention. No, it was the smallest one. Snugly sucking away at its mother's milk, no bigger than my fist, was a wee white soul with a black patch covering the right eye, which looked right at me. All I could say was, 'My, you're so tiny!'

I gently laid the other wee mite beside his mother and looked round the camp. I told Bella my folks had lived their early years in a bowed camp. I was surprised to see how well constructed it was. Despite there being no man, these two women certainly knew their stuff.

Later, while sitting around my family campfire getting tucked into tasty stovies, I told Mum all about my new-found friends, and the pups of course.

'Don't you be bothering folk, now, Jess. I saw that old woman, and she didn't look in the best of health. Give her peace, and don't be running in and out of the camp minding pups.'

As I washed before bed, I promised my mother that I would do as she said. That night I filled my dreams with the bonnie, wee, tottie dog that slept beneath the canvas of the old bowed camp, and not only that, I dreamed that he was mine.

During the next week the strawberry picking was in full swing, and wherever I went three red-headed little ones came with me. The pups grew strong, and I became more and more attached to Tiny. But when I mentioned him to Mum, she said, 'No!'

'Keeping a dog in a house is fine enough, but it would be cruel in a bus,' she said, and then added, 'I'd be forever tramping on the animal.'

Saturday morning after breakfast, I skipped off to take my new-found pals out to play. Strange it was, when I arrived, to see the fire not lit. And why was the old woman not up and about? I stood at the closed camp doorway and quietly called on Isa.

'Wait there, Jess, I'll be out in a minute,' she answered. After a while she appeared, and I could see she'd been crying.

'Is there something wrong with one of the kids?' I asked, concerned. She didn't answer, because a moan from within the camp had her dashing back inside. My concern had me intruding, as I gently bent down and pulled back the door. 'Can I help, what's wrong?' I asked again.

'Mum isn't the best this morning, lass. Do you think you could away and fetch your mother for me?' Isa looked frightened. I had seen that look before whenever folks were really poorly.

As fast as my legs could carry me, I ran home. Mum was busy washing and was up to her elbows in soapsuds. 'Old Bella's not well this morning,' I told her, 'her daughter Isa is asking for your help.' I was out of breath.

Mum could see something was seriously wrong. She quietly stopped her chores, dried her hands and took off her wet apron. 'Now, Jess,' she said softly, 'you dress the kids and light a fire, fill Isa's kettle and put it over the heat to boil.'

Without question I obeyed my mother. I then took the bewildered little ones up to our bus, where I gave them each a plate of porridge. After I had wiped little Florrie's face, we all went back to see how Bella was progressing.

'Come in, one at a time,' said my mother.

I was puzzled, what was wrong? I had enough sense, though, to see that this was adults' ways of doing. So, without question, I ushered each of them in, then out, before asking if I could come in too. Mum took my hand, pulling me onto my knees as I entered. The old woman's colour was drained white. Isa was sobbing into a flannel cloth, at the same time holding her mother's hand to her face.

Bella turned slowly to look at me. With a faint gesture she pointed to her feet where the old dog and her sleeping pups lay. 'Take the one with the black patch, bonny Jess, it's yours,' she said in a whisper.

I looked at my mother and she nodded. I was confused yet overjoyed. She had been adamant about no dogs, yet here she was, giving approval for the very thing that up till then had been denied.

She ushered me out, saying in a whisper, 'Take the wee ones away to play. At dinnertime take them up and feed them at the bus with soup from the big pot.' Before I could question her as to why it was necessary to keep them away, she added, 'Here's some money, buy sweeties.'

All I could think was, this poor old woman must be awfy sickly if I'm getting all this money for sweeties. Little did I, or the children, know just how sick Bella really was.

We played hide-and-seek in the high berry drills, stopping every now and then to pop a juicy berry in our mouths, laughing at the way the red juice ran down our cheeks. Soon we forgot about the drama back in the bowed camp as, like kids the world over, we played.

Soon, though, they tired of eating berries and playing in the high drills. So with the money Mum gave me I knew the very thing that would bring smiles, a lovely big tin of condensed milk. Off to the bothy shop I went with our pennies and my wee flock following behind, to devour the contents of heaven itself. But as we sat in a circle on a patch of clover, it dawned on me we needed a tin-opener. I told my flock of hungry kids we'd have to go back to the bus and get one.

'Not necessary,' said Clara, 'I have the very thing.' Pushing her thin fingers into a concealed pocket in her shorts, she pulled out a rusty nail. Without a word she ran her hand across the ground and picked up a medium-sized stone.

'Well done,' I said, as I hammered the dirty nail into the top of the tin.

In no time the thick, sweet, glue-like milk was spewing from the holes, and each of us in turn sucked and licked to our heart's content. Florrie, though, because of her age, just hadn't mastered the art of sooking. This resulted in half her ration disappearing up her nose. We were in fits of giggles watching her wee tongue try to lick the contents of her nose along with the sweet, creamy milk.

When time came to eat my mother's big pot of soup they had little appetite. Hardly surprising, really.

By late afternoon they were all played out and wearied for their mother. I had no choice but to take them home. 'Perhaps the hours of peace from the kids will have done Bella good, and she'd be a little better,' I thought.

But when I saw the fire still out, I thought she'd be much the same. At the camp door I told the kids to wait until I checked if it was alright to go in. Gently pulling back the door-cover, I whispered, 'Is it alright if I come in?'

'Here, Jess,' said my mother, handing me a cardboard box with four sleepy pups in it, huddled together. I did as I was told and put the puppy box down on the grass.

Isa came out, said nothing and reached for her children, holding them tightly. I looked over her head at a sight that comes vividly into my mind even now. Bella was covered over by a blanket. Unable to stop myself I pulled the cover from her face. 'She'll suffocate,' I shouted.

Mum squeezed my hand and whispered in my ear that Bella had died, and then lifted me away from the old woman's death-bed. I took one last look before dashing outside. She was grey-coloured. Her eyelids half shut, chin resting on her chest. So this was how dead folks looked!

My mother slipped her arm through mine and said, 'Come now, pet, let's leave this family to their grief.' She then added, 'I'll have to get homes for these pups.' I wondered why she didn't take the bitch as well, and asked her so.

'The strangest thing,' she said, 'the minute the old woman went, the bitch went with her. That old dog just gave a heavy sigh, stretched her legs and died!'

Thinking on my mother's previous promise I peered into the box to see if Tiny was still there. 'You're not giving my wee one away, are you Mum?' I asked, thinking she had only said it to keep the dying woman content.

'No, don't fret, lass, you should know me better than that – a promise must be kept. But remember this, I don't want to see a squashed pup under the bus wheels or an accidentally kicked one rushing around the bus. You now have a dog, so take care of it.'

Tiny became our beloved family pet. Dad took him away when he went to work, I took him playing among the hills and glens. He was there when my oldest sister got married and there when my youngest did too.

You may find this difficult to believe, but when he passed away, our Tiny was 21 years old!

Well, like all good things, even stories must end. Sharing all these tales with you has been great fun. I hope now that you have spent some time with me, you might have a better understanding of the ways of the travelling people.

Before our culture is gone for ever, I would like to think that we may be remembered fondly for one thing – our truly wonderful stories that we have so carefully passed down from one generation to another. They are yours now, so guard them well...